Rosie put her hands on her hips. "I'm not going to the Pop Stop with Heather," she said. "She could really hurt our chances of becoming popular. She's...you know...nerdy."

"She's *not* nerdy," I replied. "And if you would just spend some time with her, you'd know that."

Rosie tossed her head and crossed her arms. "If you ask me, you're spending way *too much* time with her."

"No more than you spend with Shannon."

Rosie's expression softened. "Hey, we're in junior high now. We finally have a chance to be part of the popular crowd. Don't you want that?"

"No, I don't."

"Well, I do," Rosie said, her voice rising. "You're going to have to choose who you'd rather be friends with. So which is it, Amy—me or Heather?"

**Get the inside scoop from
DIARY S.O.S.**

I've Lost My Best Friend

by Megan Howard

BULLSEYE BOOKS

Random House 🏠 New York

To Bruce

A BULLSEYE BOOK PUBLISHED BY RANDOM HOUSE, INC.

Produced by Daniel Weiss Associates, Inc.,
33 West 17th Street, New York, NY 10011.

Library of Congress Catalog Card Number: 93-85681
ISBN: 0-679-85701-X

RL: 4.8

First Bullseye Books edition: April 1994

Manufactured in the United States of America   10 9 8 7 6 5 4 3 2 1

New York, Toronto, London, Sydney, Auckland

Chapter 1

Dear Diary,

    Grandma gave me this diary for my twelfth birthday way back in February, but I haven't used it until today. Now that I'm about to enter seventh grade and so many things are changing, I've decided to start writing my thoughts down. So here goes!

    Tomorrow is my first day at Whitman Junior High School and I'm kind of scared about it. Well, "kind of" is putting it mildly. The truth is my stomach is full of butterflies. I went to Cunningham Park Elementary for seven years! I knew practically everyone there. Now I have to start all over again-new building, new teachers, new classes, new kids.

    And I'm sure the work is going to be a

lot harder. I'm not exactly the world's best student, so that kind of worries me. At least they still have phys ed — my favorite subject — and real sports teams.

I'm lucky that my best friend Rosie will be there to help me out. Well, by this time tomorrow I'll know all about junior high.

— Amy the seventh grader

"Can you believe it?" Rosie Banton asked as she twirled around the room in new black leggings and a purple blouse that still had the price tag dangling from one of the sleeves. "Tomorrow we'll officially be seventh graders!"

I looked up from the *Athlete's Monthly* magazine that I was reading on Rosie's bed. "Yeah — seventh graders getting up at seven A.M. and doing homework all night. I can't wait!" I made a gagging sound for emphasis.

"Don't remind me," she said in her lilting Jamaican accent. "Homework is one thing about seventh grade I'm definitely *not* looking forward to."

"There are a lot of things about junior high that I'm dreading."

Rosie arched her eyebrows as she slid a tiny gold hoop earring into her ear. "Like what? I thought you were happy we're finally starting at Whitman."

"That was when it didn't seem so real—when we were riding our bikes or hanging out at the pool." I sighed as I thought about all the fun we had over the summer. "But we're not going to be able to just do nothing again for an entire school year."

"You're right about that," Rosie said as she sat down next to me on her purple comforter. Purple is Rosie's favorite color, so everything in her room is purple—the walls, rug, lamps…everything. "This was definitely the best summer ever. But I still think Whitman's going to be really cool. Different classes, clubs…and cute guys!"

"How do you know the guys are going to be cuter than the ones at Cunningham Park?"

"Yvonne told me. She remembers the guys in junior high as being the cutest." Yvonne is one of Rosie's sisters. She had gone away to college just a week ago, and already Rosie had called her at least five times.

"Is that what you're going to wear tomorrow?" I asked, changing the subject. Cute or not, I don't care about guys as much as Rosie does.

Rosie's dark brown eyes examined her reflection in the full-length mirror on the closet door. Her curly brown hair is cut close-cropped, shorter than my ten-year-old brother Simon's, but Rosie doesn't look like a boy at all. Instead, the hairstyle shows off her dark, exotic features. Her eyes are surrounded by long eyelashes and dramatic black eyebrows. Her lips are full and, well, rosy, as if she were wearing lipstick (which is impossible, because Rosie's parents never let her wear any makeup).

"What do you think? Does it look good on me?" she asked. She turned sideways to look at the blouse from a different angle.

I tried not to roll my eyes, but I couldn't help letting out a big sigh. Rosie had been trying on different outfits for more than an hour already.

"Rosie, it looks great on you. Everything does. In fact, you could have worn any one of the twenty outfits you've already tried on."

Rosie nodded at the mirror. "Okay, I'll wear this tomorrow and the overalls the next day," she said. "Now we have to figure out what *you're* going to wear." She studied me as though she had never seen me before. "Jeans and a T-shirt?"

I always wear jeans and a T-shirt, unless I'm wearing shorts and a T-shirt, or jeans and a sweater.

"I was hoping you would say that. But which T-shirt?"

"How about the purple one with the sailboat that we got at Virginia Beach? Then we'll kind of match."

"I'll wear my black hightops, too."

"Perfect. I'll borrow Anne's black sandals."

"Not unless you ask!" Rosie's sister Anne shouted from the hallway. She's in high school, and just about the only time that she and Rosie speak to each other is when they're fighting about clothes.

Rosie raced to her bedroom door and threw it open so that she could see Anne.

"You shouldn't be eavesdropping," Rosie warned her sister.

"It's a good thing I was, or you would have taken my sandals without asking."

"Come on, it's just one time."

Anne tapped her chin with her index finger. "Perhaps we can work something out," she said slyly.

"I'll clean your closet," Rosie offered without hesitating.

"And my dresser drawers," Anne added.

"It's a deal!" the girls said in unison, and shook hands.

I smiled. Ever since the Bantons had moved from Jamaica into the house next door to mine four years ago, I had seen Rosie and Anne bargain this way. In the end, Rosie always got to borrow whatever she wanted, and Anne managed to get Rosie to do her chores, clean her bedroom, or wash her new car.

"Don't forget what I told you," Anne said, looking at me. "If you get lost—"

"I know, I know," I said. "Don't ask an eighth grader for directions." Anne had gone to Whitman too. All summer she'd been warning Rosie and me that if we asked the older kids for directions, they'd probably send us searching for an elevator that didn't exist or walking around in circles.

"Right." She gave me a thumbs-up, smiled, and walked off to her bedroom.

I looked at Rosie's clock. "Oops! I've got to go. I'm late for dinner. Simon's probably eaten everything by now." I grabbed my magazine and headed for the door.

"I'll be at your house tomorrow at seven-thirty," Rosie shouted as I went down the stairs.

"I want to be early for the first day."

I turned around and smiled. "I'll be ready!"

As I walked out the Bantons' front door I was actually almost looking forward to my first day at Walt Whitman Junior High.

"*Aaa*-my." Rosie's accent rose above the roar of kids in the lunchroom. "Over here!" I turned to my left and finally spotted Rosie standing on the far side of the cafeteria, furiously waving her arms to get my attention.

"I thought I'd never find you," I told Rosie, putting my wilted lunch bag on the table. "I've never seen so many kids before." I pulled out the chair next to her and sat down.

"I know. Isn't it great? What took you so long?" she asked, sipping her milk shake. She had already been through the lunch line. Since I always bring my lunch, I didn't have to buy anything.

"My math class is way over on the other side of the building," I explained. Then I mumbled, "And I asked an eighth grader for directions."

"Oh, no!" Rosie groaned. "You didn't!" I scrunched my nose and nodded, then both of us laughed.

"At least you made it before lunch was over,"

Rosie teased, shaking her head. She was used to my lateness. That morning when she came by to pick me up at seven-thirty, I wasn't even halfway ready.

"Anyway, I wouldn't have found it any faster on my own," I explained. "I'll never get used to this place."

"You'll figure it out eventually. The only reason I can find my way around is because I've been here a million times for Anne's school plays and orchestra concerts."

"I'm not sure I like junior high," I lamented, putting my chin in my hand.

"Why?" Rosie asked, concerned.

"We have only two classes together."

"That's true. But this way it's perfect," she said, nudging me with her elbow. "I'll help you in science, and you help me in PE. If you think about it, we really lucked out."

"Yeah. Wasn't volleyball great this morning?" I asked, pulling my lunch out of the bag.

"Sure," she agreed, then added, "if you like sweating first thing in the morning. Anyway, you've got to look on the bright side," Rosie explained. "Junior high is way better than elementary."

"How do you figure?"

"For one thing," she went on, "we get to eat at whatever lunch table we want, and—"

A loud crash interrupted our conversation. A muscular boy with light brown hair—obviously one of the cute ones Yvonne had told Rosie about—had knocked into Karen Patel, a girl from my math class. Her tray had slipped out of her hands and landed on the floor. Peas were rolling in all directions, and an eighth-grade science book lay next to a puddle of gravy. I pushed my chair out to help Karen, but before I could get out of my seat, a custodian had rushed to the scene with a mop. Then, to my amazement, the boy handed Karen his own lunch tray. "Sorry," he said. "My fault." He picked up his book and went back to stand in the lunch line again.

"Did you see that?" I asked, settling back in my seat. After all Anne had told us, I was surprised to see an eighth grader being so nice—especially to a seventh grader.

"Are you kidding?" Rosie answered, her eyes still glued to the guy. "What a hunk. That's the cutest guy I've seen in my life."

"Oh, Rosie, can't you think of anything else? I was talking about the fact that he was so nice, giving up his own lunch and all."

"Well, as I was saying, there are tons of good things about junior high," Rosie continued. "Besides the cute guys, we get to have our own lockers instead of sharing a tiny coat closet with everyone else."

I smiled. "And I can keep mine as neat as I want," I added.

"Don't you mean as messy as you want?" Rosie teased.

"And Whitman has real sports teams," I continued, ignoring her comment. "Track tryouts are coming up soon. I've got to start training right now if I'm going to make the team."

"Amy, you don't have a thing to worry about." Rosie pushed her tray to one side. She'd eaten only half her sandwich and a few potato chips. "You were the fastest runner at Cunningham Park—boy or girl."

"I can't take any chances," I told her. "Only a few seventh graders make the team. Anyway, there wasn't much competition at Cunningham Park."

Rosie crossed her arms in front of her and shook her head. "You're going to get all worked up about it; then, you'll come in first place and wish you hadn't made yourself so sick." Sometimes Rosie knows me better than I know myself. But the Whitman coaches didn't know me, and wouldn't necessarily be as confident about my abilities as my best friend was. Anyway, I'd find out at tryouts.

"Look at all these kids," I said. "I feel like I hardly know anyone here. I can't wait to meet everyone in my classes."

"Mmm hmm," Rosie agreed as she scanned the crowd.

"Look, there's Lucy." I pointed to where Lucy Cruz, a girl who lives down the street from us, was sitting with her friends. She waved.

"Want to go sit with them?" I asked Rosie.

"Uh, no."

I looked at her suspiciously. "Why not?"

"I just don't want to sit in the middle of the cafeteria. From over here we get a better view."

"Of what?" I asked Rosie.

"Who's in the right crowd." By now Rosie wasn't looking at me anymore. She was back to studying the students around us.

"You can't be serious," I said, shaking my head so that my blond ponytail slapped my shoulders.

Rosie looked right at me. "This is our year to start fresh, to find out who's in the most popular group and make friends with them."

"What if we don't like the most popular kids?"

"People aren't popular unless they're well-liked," Rosie said in a tone that meant she was through talking about it.

I rolled my eyes. Being in junior high obviously hadn't softened her stubborn streak.

"I've already started to get to know some of the most popular girls," Rosie continued. "I sat near them in a couple of my classes and got great information about where they hang out and what clubs they're joining. Some of them are going to be on the pep squad."

"What's that?"

"A group of kids go who go to all the sports events and sit in the bleachers and cheer." Rosie turned toward me. "So I'll be there for your track meets this season and basketball games in the winter."

"That sounds like a good idea," I said, taking a sip of apple juice. "Who's in that crowd?"

"Shannon Sommer."

I nearly spit my juice across the table! Shannon had gone to another elementary school, but I knew her from the pool and the Pop Stop, the big Englewood hangout. Every inch of Shannon is perfect. She has long blond hair that falls in waves down her back. And she was the only girl I know who was allowed to wear makeup in sixth grade. Shannon's only imperfection is her personality. She's a big snob and always makes mean remarks about people who aren't in her clique.

I swallowed the juice and regained my composure. "Shannon's never even spoken to us," I reminded Rosie.

"She talked to me today in English."

"About what?"

"She asked to borrow a pencil." Then Rosie quickly added, "But she could have asked anyone in the class."

I leaned my head to the side and looked at Rosie. In my opinion, phony people like Shannon had a very special way of choosing friends, usually based on looks and clothes. I knew I could never meet her standards, and I didn't think I wanted to try.

I had to admit, though, Rosie might look better with Shannon's crowd than with a tomboy like me. Unlike me, Rosie never gets pimples, and her figure is a lot more developed than most of the seventh-grade girls I know. Compared to Shannon and Rosie, I'm a stick with hair—long, stringy blond hair.

Behind Rosie someone sneezed, but the sound was more like a mouse squeak. I peered over Rosie's shoulder. A small girl with chin-length brown hair and glasses was sitting all alone at the end of our table, reading a book.

"Maybe we should ask her to sit with us," I whispered to Rosie, pointing in the girl's direction.

Rosie turned around in her seat. "She looks pretty serious."

"That's probably because she doesn't have anyone to talk to. I'm going to invite her over."

I walked to the end of the table. Close up the girl looked much younger than most of the other kids at Whitman. She had round cheeks and a small nose. I tapped her on the shoulder. She looked up from her book and pushed her glasses up on her nose.

"Hi, I'm Amy Leonard. I was wondering if you'd like to sit with my friend Rosie and me." I motioned toward Rosie.

"Um, thanks," she said. Her cheeks got a little pinker. "But I've got to read this book for English." She spoke quietly and barely looked in my direction.

"It's the first day of school. Your teacher

can't expect you to spend your lunch working."

The shy girl shrugged and closed her book. "Yeah, I guess you're right. My name's Heather Cohen."

Chapter 2

"Where do you live?" I asked once Heather sat down.

Heather stared at her folded hands in her lap. "Plum Street."

"Hey, that's just a couple blocks away from Rosie and me. We're on Cottage."

Heather shifted in her seat. "Oh…good."

"When did you move in?"

"Two weeks ago."

I wanted to let Heather know that she didn't have to be self-conscious around us, but I didn't know how to tell her without embarrassing her.

I turned to Rosie and gave her my best pleading look. She came to my rescue. "So…what classes do you have after lunch?"

Heather pulled a piece of paper out of the book she had been reading. "Next is math. Then social studies. And science."

"Are you in Mr. Norris's science class?" Rosie asked.

"Yes."

"That's great!" I said. "We are too."

"My sister Anne says that Mr. Norris is the best teacher," Rosie informed Heather. "He's tough, but fun."

Heather nodded slightly, her eyes cast down at the table.

"Do you like science?" Rosie asked.

"Mmm hmm. I like English better, though."

"Next to science, English is my worst subject," I told Heather.

"Yeah, they can be pretty hard." Then for the first time Heather looked me directly in the eyes. "Well, I'd better go. I'll see you in sixth period." She pushed her chair away from the table and got up. Rosie and I said good-bye to Heather and watched her hurry out of the lunchroom.

"I don't think she likes us," Rosie said as the doors closed behind Heather.

"I think she's just a little shy."

"Maybe, but it seemed that she really wanted to get away from us."

"I'm sure it just looked that way because she's nervous about being in a new school with a bunch of kids she doesn't even know. She'll probably change once she meets people."

Rosie shrugged. She stood to pick up her lunch tray. "I need to stop by my locker before public speaking. You want to come with me?"

I looked down at the dinner leftovers in front of me. My mother has her own catering business, so she's used to making lots of food at once. Sometimes she gets carried away when she's cooking for my family, and we have to eat leftovers for an entire week.

"I'd better finish my lunch."

"Okay. I'll try to save you a seat in sixth period. Don't be *too* late!"

In fourth-period social studies, Claudia Reeves sat down at the desk next to mine.

"I didn't think I'd know anyone in this class," I said, relieved to see a familiar face.

Claudia and I had played on the same softball team over the summer—the Rams. She's about as tall I am, but at least thirty pounds heavier. Not only was she the best pitcher in the league, but she was also the friendliest player. She got to know just about all the players on every team.

Claudia looked around the room. "I don't

know anyone else either. Are all of these kids from Englewood?"

"I guess a lot of them are from Williamston, too," I told her. Williamston is the town next to Englewood. My father moved there after my parents got divorced three years ago. Kids from Williamston ride the bus to school.

"So, have you decided which sports you're going to play?" Claudia asked.

I nodded. "Track...well, at least I *hope* I make the team. I'm going to stay after school to work out with the eighth graders."

"Me too. I want to compete in the field events," she added. "My brother thinks I might be able to throw the shot put or discus." I had seen those events in track-and-field competitions on TV, but I had never actually tried either of them. I knew the shot put was sort of like a lead softball, and the discus was like a lead plate.

The late bell rang, and a couple of panicked students hurried down the hall. Mrs. Goldman was talking to another teacher, so she didn't come in right away.

Instead, Shannon Sommer sauntered into the room and sat down in the last empty seat, right next to me. She was wearing a red polka dot sundress and looked incredibly bored as she twisted her long hair up on her head, then let it fall on her back. She sighed heavily and began writing her name on all of her notebooks.

Shannon looked as lonely as I had been before Claudia sat down next to me. I felt kind of sorry for her. Shannon just didn't look right without lots of friends and admirers around her. *Maybe I was wrong about Shannon*, I thought. *She looks as if she might want someone to talk to.*

"Hi. I'm Amy, and this is my friend Claudia."

Shannon stopped writing and turned her head in my direction. "Oh," she said. Then she faced forward, rolled her eyes, and let out another sigh. This time, though, it sounded fake and forced.

I felt as if Shannon had slam-dunked me through a basketball hoop. As far as she was concerned, the conversation was over. Either she figured everyone already knew who she was, or she didn't want *us* to know.

"Shannon, didn't you see us?" A high voice from the back of the room called out. "We saved you a seat."

Quickly Shannon turned around, her golden hair nearly whipping me across the face. "I'm so glad you guys are here," Shannon said, then glanced over at me. She grabbed her books and hurried to the back of the classroom to join her friends.

"Psst!" Claudia said to get my attention. When I turned toward her, she held the tip of her nose high in the air, pursed her lips, and swayed her body back and forth.

When the teacher, Mrs. Goldman, finally entered the room, I struggled to hold back my giggles as Claudia sat up straight in her chair and tried to look innocent.

I hated to break it to Rosie, but it didn't look as if Shannon wanted me in her crowd.

A stack of papers landed with a thud on the table where Rosie and I were sitting. At first I thought Mr. Norris did it to wake me out of my daydream. Then I noticed that he was dropping a pile on every table in the front row. Rosie had arrived before anyone else had and saved us seats at the table right in front of Mr. Norris's desk.

"Please take one and pass back the rest," he instructed us. "I'll start to explain some of the equipment pictured on the second page of your information packet."

Mr. Norris wore a suit and a bow tie. He had

gray hair and spoke with an accent. I tried to concentrate on what he was saying, but I was having a lot of trouble. My mind kept wandering.

First, I timed how long Rosie stared at our teacher without blinking. Two minutes, thirty-seven seconds. Rosie usually reserved that kind of attention for movie stars and cute guys. Mr. Norris was neither of these things. He was a scientist, though, and Rosie was crazy about science.

Then I checked to see how many kids in the class had gone to Cunningham Park Elementary. I noticed Heather sitting a couple of tables away, looking around the room uncomfortably. *It must be horrible not to know anyone in the whole school*, I thought. It was bad enough for me, knowing only a few kids in the class.

I smiled at her, and for the first time since I'd introduced myself she smiled back.

"With the remaining time," Mr. Norris said, interrupting my thoughts—he'd finished going over the packet, and I hadn't heard one word—"I'd like to get started with a science lab to get you used to experimental procedures."

"On the first day of school?" Aaron Greenberg, who was the biggest blabbermouth at

Cunningham Park, moaned loudly.

Mr. Norris looked at Aaron over his glasses. "I'd be happy to let you complete yours in detention if you prefer."

"Nnn-no, that's okay," Aaron stammered. "I was just making sure I heard you right."

"I will speak very clearly from now on so that there will be no confusion." Mr. Norris exaggerated the pronunciation of each word.

I had to admit I agreed with Aaron. The least Mr. Norris could have done was give us a chance to get used to the idea of doing a lab. Panic crept through me.

"You will be working in pairs," our teacher announced.

"Excellent!" Rosie and I said at the same time as the other kids began talking and scrambling to claim their partners.

Then Mr. Norris clapped his hands to get the class's attention. "Your lab partner should be someone you did not know before today."

I felt the blood rush from my face as he made the announcement.

"Sorry," Rosie said sympathetically. "I guess I won't be able to help you out."

"Yeah, well maybe Heather wants to work with me."

Chapter 3

"What's this?" I asked Heather, as I pointed to what looked like a metal candle.

Heather looked up from the lab instructions that Mr. Norris had given us. "Um…it's a Bunsen burner." She looked down again and wrote something on the top of the paper.

"What's it for?"

"To cook or melt things."

"Sounds like home economics, not science," I joked.

To my surprise, Heather actually laughed.

"First, we're supposed to write a message on a piece of paper using the cotton swab," she explained.

I stared at the Q-tip and the cup of lemon juice on the table and waited for Heather to write something.

"Well, go ahead," Heather coaxed.

"You want *me* to do it?" I asked. Heather nodded. "I'm not very good at science. I'll probably mess it up." Whenever Rosie and I worked together, she usually did the experiment and explained the results to me.

"How could you mess it up? Just write whatever you want," Heather said. "Don't tell me, though. I want it to be a surprise."

I adjusted my plastic goggles and thought about what to write. Then I dipped the swab in the juice. "I just don't understand how lemon juice can be invisible ink," I told Heather as I dragged the Q-tip across the paper. "It's juice, not magic."

Heather shrugged and lit the Bunsen burner. "Maybe that's why he assigned this lab," she said. "To show us that science can be fun."

"That's easy to say if you're a science nut, like you or Rosie."

I looked over at Rosie, who was working a couple of tables away, and it didn't look as if she was having too much fun right now. As a matter of fact, she looked pretty miserable. Her partner was a guy named Glen Benedict, who was tall and skinny with short black hair and ears that stuck way out.

"Next we're supposed to hold the paper over

the flame and see what happens," Heather announced, reminding me that I had my own lab to worry about. I lifted the paper off the table. "Make sure you hold the paper high enough so that it doesn't catch fire," Heather read from the instruction sheet.

I nodded and carefully moved the secret message over the flame. Heather and I watched as the letters slowly appeared.

"'Welcome to Englewood,'" Heather read, smiling. She shyly looked down at the floor. "Thanks."

"I get it!" I called out. "The heat from the Bunsen burner cooked the lemon juice."

Suddenly, there was a scream from the next table. Glen was flapping his arms and frantically running in a circle around a flaming piece of paper lying on the floor. Rosie quickly filled a beaker with water and poured it over the flames.

By the time Mr. Norris rushed over to their table, the fire was out. "You handled that very well, Miss Banton," he said, patting Rosie on the shoulder. "Fortunately it was just a paper fire, so you were able to douse it with water. A chemical fire could have caused serious problems." He looked over his glasses at Glen. "I wish everyone kept such a cool head in an emergency."

When Rosie looked over at me, I gave her a big smile to cheer her up. I knew she must have hated messing up on the very first day of her favorite class.

After I carried the Bunsen burner to the cabinet and returned to our table, which Heather had just finished cleaning, the bell rang. "I can't believe sixth period's over already!" I told Heather.

"Yeah, the time really flew. Thanks for your help."

"*You're* thanking *me*?" I asked. "I probably would have skipped a couple steps or something without you."

Heather picked up her science notebook. "Maybe we can be lab partners again."

"That would be great!"

When I returned to my table, Rosie was holding her books in her arms, ready to leave. I picked up my backpack, and we walked into the noisy hall full of kids. "Heather's really great at science," I told Rosie. "She was in a special science club at her old school, and they did really neat experiments and went on field trips."

"She actually told you all that? She seemed so shy at lunch."

"Yeah. She was really quiet at first, but then when we started working on the lab, she loosened up."

"You really lucked out working with her," Rosie said. "Next time if *we* can't be lab partners, I get Heather and you have to have Glen."

"Thanks for being so generous," I said sarcastically.

"What are best friends for?" Rosie asked, laughing. "Come on. My locker's up here." We followed the mass of kids going up the stairs to the second floor.

As we turned the corner at the top of the stairwell, I saw Heather searching through the locker right next to Rosie's. "Hi, Heather," Rosie said when we got to her locker.

"Oh, hi, you guys," Heather answered quietly.

"So how'd you like your first day at Whitman?" Rosie asked.

Heather put a thick math book in her already packed book bag. "It was all right, I guess. The kids seem pretty nice."

"Do you want to walk home with us?" I asked.

"No, thanks," Heather said, hesitating a little. "My mom's picking me up." Her cheeks turned red, and she looked down at her shoes. She shouldn't have been embarrassed, though. She was incredibly lucky, if you ask me. Rosie and I hardly ever got a ride home from school.

Heather shut her locker and slid her red-and-white book bag strap onto her shoulder. I was afraid she'd topple over from its weight.

"I'll see you tomorrow," she said.

When Heather was out of sight, Rosie said, "I definitely don't think she likes me."

"Why?"

"For one thing, she rushed off as soon as I got here even though she talked to you in science."

"She didn't talk to me much either. Her mother was probably waiting for her."

"That's the other thing. Why didn't she offer to give us a ride home? You told her we were on the way."

I shrugged. "I don't know. Maybe she and her mom are going somewhere besides their house...or maybe they don't have enough room in the car. Besides, she barely knows us."

Rosie gave me a sideways look. "I don't know," she said as she opened her locker. "I think there's something funny going on with that girl."

By now most of the kids had left, and there were just a few stragglers talking to friends or getting books out of their lockers. Unfortunately, Shannon and three of her friends were there—and they were walking in our direction. I didn't want to give Shannon the satisfaction of knowing that I'd seen her, so I quickly turned my back to her.

"Rosie, thanks for jumping in for me on that math question today." Shannon had stopped right behind me to talk to Rosie! "I could barely stay awake. Miss Cooley is *so* boring." I had Miss Cooley in third period. She was taller than my dad and had a booming voice. Even though I really don't like math, I had found it hard not to pay attention.

Rosie flicked her hand. "Forget it. You probably would have done the same for me."

Don't bet on it, I said silently, waiting for Shannon to notice that I was standing next to her new friend.

"Hey, I saw that new girl Heather talking to you," Shannon went on. She made a face. "You're not friends with her, are you?"

"Oh…uh…not really," Rosie said.

"Good. She lives next door to me. Her dog is always coming into our yard and chasing our cat, and I can't get her to do anything about it. My dad had to get Peaches down from the roof with a ladder the other day."

Rosie shook her head.

"She sure is weird," one of Shannon's friends added. "Who spends the entire first day of school with her nose in a book?"

Rosie just shrugged.

"I'll save you a seat in English tomorrow, Rosie," Shannon said as she moved away. Finally, she noticed me standing right next to Rosie. She stopped, looked me up and down, and went on without another word.

Rosie grabbed her jacket out of her locker. She was smiling as though she'd just been crowned queen of the world.

"What was that all about?" I asked.

"Oh, I guess I forgot to tell you. We have math together fifth period. Miss Cooley called on Shannon when she wasn't paying attention." Rosie shrugged and shut her locker. "So I answered the question."

"You pretended you were Shannon?" I asked

Rosie as we walked down the hall.

"No, Miss Cooley knew I wasn't Shannon, but she didn't say anything about it."

"You shouldn't get in trouble for that snob," I told Rosie as we turned the corner and headed down the stairwell to the first floor.

"Don't worry about it. By tomorrow Miss Cooley won't even remember what happened. Besides, I cover for you all the time."

It was true. Rosie had covered for me lots of times when my mind had wandered in class. Still, I hated to be compared with Shannon. Rosie and I had been best friends for four years. She'd known Shannon only a day.

"I have to tell you what happened in social studies," I said.

Rosie immediately looked interested. "Did you meet a cute guy?"

"No, not exactly." I told her about the way that Shannon had snubbed Claudia and me. Then I waited for Rosie to take my side and announce that she'd never talk to Shannon again.

Rosie put a hand on my shoulder. "I'm sure that Shannon didn't mean to be snobby. She's really pretty nice."

"So why did she ignore me just now?" I

asked, switching my backpack to the opposite shoulder.

Rosie leaned her head to the side and looked at me sympathetically. "Because her friends were waiting for her. Come on, Amy. It's not such a big deal. Once we're in her crowd, you'll see how wrong you are about her."

I let out an exasperated sigh as we walked outside.

"Why wouldn't she like you, anyway? You're the nicest, funniest, best person I know!" Rosie added. Then she spotted Lucy and hurried toward her.

Maybe because I'm not the prettiest *person you know,* I answered silently.

Dear Diary,

I actually made it through the first day of school! It's not as bad as I thought it would be. (Except for the fact that my math teacher already gave us homework!)

There's just one problem, though. Rosie doesn't like my new friend, Heather Cohen, and she's convinced that Heather doesn't like her either.

Well, I don't know how she can want to be friends with snobby Shannon Sommer

instead of Heather, but I've got this idea.
If I can get Heather to open up around
Rosie, Rosie will see how great Heather is.
(Now I just have to come up with a plan.)
                                    -Gotta go, Amy

Chapter 4

I checked my watch as I raced past the school's main office after math on Friday. *Excellent!* I complimented myself. *Two minutes ahead of schedule.*

Earlier in the week, Rosie and I had agreed to meet by her locker every day before lunch. She had suggested it, because for two days in a row she was nearly finished eating by the time I made it to the cafeteria.

I raced up to the second floor, taking the steps two at a time, then peered down the hall. *No Rosie*, I thought, panting. I couldn't wait to see her reaction when she arrived to find *me* waiting for *her.*

Up ahead I saw Heather putting her books into her locker. I hadn't invited her to lunch since the first day of school because Rosie hadn't changed her mind about being friends with her. And Mr. Norris hadn't assigned any more labs, so there hadn't been a chance for us to work together again in science class.

As I passed Heather's locker I peeked inside. It was the most organized space I'd ever seen in my life! Even my mother doesn't keep her closets and drawers that neat, and she's a real neat freak.

Then I saw something that surprised me even more. Taped to the inside of the door was a picture of one of the cutest guys I'd ever seen. He had wavy brown hair that hung over his forehead, but you could still see his blue eyes. Even more amazing were his dimples and incredibly white teeth. In the lower right-hand corner of the photo the words TO HEATHER, WITH LOVE, DONNY were written in black Magic Marker.

"Is that your boyfriend?" I asked, impressed.

I guess my voice startled her, because Heather jumped. "What did you say?" she asked, once she'd gotten over the shock.

I pointed to the picture and repeated my question.

"Are you kidding?" Heather laughed. "That's Donny Davenport."

"Who?"

"You know, from that TV show *One Big Family*. He plays the oldest brother."

"Oh, yeah! He's Rosie's favorite actor."

"Really? I could get her a picture too."

"Wow! That would be great," I said. "So how did you get a picture of a TV star? Did you meet him?"

"I wish! My mom is an entertainment writer—she does articles about TV and movies and stuff like that. She gets to interview a lot of stars."

"So she interviewed Donny Davenport?"

Heather nodded. "Mom feels bad that she gets to have all the fun, so she brings me back an autographed picture if she can. She usually gets a few extras for her files, too."

"That is so cool," I said.

Heather bent over and picked up what looked like a weird suitcase.

"What's that?" I asked.

"It's my sax."

"You play the saxophone? Wow!"

Heather looked surprised. "It's not really such a big deal."

"Well, *I* think it's really cool. Everyone I know plays the flute or the piano. Nobody plays the sax." I made a spontaneous decision. "When

Rosie gets here, do you want to go down to the cafeteria and eat lunch together?"

Heather nodded. "That'd be great!"

Just then Rosie came up behind me, huffing and puffing. "Sorry I'm late," she panted. "But Shannon—"

"Guess what!" I said, cutting Rosie off in midsentence. I didn't mean to be rude, but I had heard all I could take about Shannon for one week. Practically every other word out of Rosie's mouth lately had something to do with how spectacular Shannon or one of her crowd was. Nothing Rosie had said had convinced me that I was wrong about Shannon, and nothing could compare to my good news. "Heather plays the sax, and look—she's got an autographed picture of Donny Davenport," I blurted out.

Rosie looked at the picture on the door. I could see her eyes widen. "That's pretty neat," she said. Then she began to spin the dial on her locker.

I was disappointed that Rosie wasn't more enthusiastic about having something in common with Heather, but I wasn't about to give up. "Heather's eating lunch with us," I announced.

"Oh, that's what I was going to tell you," Rosie said apologetically. "Shannon invited me to sit at her table today."

Rosie might as well have punched me in the stomach. We had eaten school lunch together every day since the third grade, unless one of us was sick. And at that moment that was just how I was feeling.

"What about—" I began.

"Sorry, I can't talk right now. I've got to get going," she announced, piling her books on the locker shelf, then closing the door. She took off down the hall. I wanted to race after her, but I couldn't desert Heather the way that Rosie had deserted me.

"Her loss," Heather said, pulling a bag of multicolored candies out of her lunch bag. "Today I brought Fruit Goos."

The boulder in my gut shrank down to the size of a pebble. I grinned at Heather, stuck my hand into the bag she was holding in front of me, and popped a candy into my mouth.

Rosie held up a yellow shirt with a pattern of brown horses and cowboy hats dancing around on it. "Do you think this is too babyish?" she asked.

I looked up at Rosie from the purple bean-bag chair in her bedroom and shrugged. "I don't know."

My mom had to prepare a big catering event for Saturday. Whenever she worked late, I hung out at the Bantons' and Simon went to his friend Mario Gomes's house until my stepfather, Paul, got home.

I couldn't hold my disappointment about what had happened at lunch inside any longer. "Why did you run off like that today?"

Rosie replaced the yellow shirt with a blue denim one. She looked in the mirror. "I told you. I was late meeting Shannon in the cafeteria."

"But you were supposed to have lunch with me."

She turned away from the mirror and dropped the shirt on her bed. "I would have invited you, but you were already eating with Heather."

"What does that have to do with anything?"

"I just thought it would be better for everyone if Heather didn't come. You know Shannon doesn't like her."

"Next time, at least give me a chance to say something," I told her.

"I'm sorry. I guess I was in such a big hurry that I just wasn't thinking." Rosie flashed me a huge smile. "Anyway, we're together now. And we'll probably be together most of the weekend—unless you have other plans."

"No, my dad hasn't asked Simon and me to do anything special." Dad lives in the next town, so on weekends we sometimes hang out there and sometimes just stay in Englewood.

"Well, to prove how truly sorry I am, I'll buy you French fries at the Pop Stop tomorrow." The Pop Stop is one of the coolest places in Englewood—and our favorite place to hang out. Besides regular food like hamburgers and pizza, it serves about fifty different kinds of drinks.

"Deal!"

"Good. Because Shannon and the rest of the gang are going to be there. We can probably sit with them."

I frowned. My afternoon with Rosie had just become an afternoon with Shannon and her snobby friends.

"I don't think—" I began to protest, then stopped myself.

"What?" Rosie asked.

"Oh, nothing." If Rosie needed proof that Shannon didn't like me, she'd get it tomorrow.

Chapter 5

"Amy, where did you learn to set the table like that?" Paul asked from the other side of the kitchen.

I stopped what I was doing and glanced up at my stepfather. "Huh?" I asked. Then I looked down at the place in front of me. The fork and spoon were flip-flopped, and the napkin was all wadded up.

"I guess I wasn't paying attention."

"You're kidding!" Paul teased, then went back to stirring the spaghetti sauce on the stove. He likes to cook almost as much as my mother does. They met in one of the night-school cooking classes Mom sometimes teaches at Englewood High School and got married two years ago.

I fixed the utensils. But as hard as I tried to concentrate on getting the table ready, my mind kept wandering. "I've got it!" I shouted.

"Got what?" Paul asked. He lifted the spoon to sample some sauce.

"Um… nothing. I'll be right back." I bounded out of the kitchen and into the foyer, where I had dropped my backpack when I got home from Rosie's.

Paul laughed. "Hurry back as soon as you're finished doing nothing," he called after me.

I unzipped my backpack and pulled out the piece of paper on which I'd written Heather's phone number the first day of school. Then I raced downstairs to the phone in the family room.

Simon was lying on his stomach in front of the TV watching cartoons. "I have to use the phone for a while. Can you leave?"

"What will you pay me?" he asked.

I grinned like the villain in his cartoon. "I won't tell Molly Packard that you like her." Molly lives about four houses away from us and has a big crush on Simon.

"I *don't* like her!"

"She doesn't know that."

Simon stomped up the stairs, pouting. When he reached the top he called down, "Tell me when you're through."

"I will. It won't take very long."

The phone rang three times before someone picked up. "Hello?" I recognized Heather's quiet voice right away.

"Hi, Heather. It's Amy."

"Hi, Amy." She sounded surprised to hear from me. "What's up?"

"Rosie and I are going to the Pop Stop tomorrow, and I wondered if you want to come."

"I heard some people at school talking about the Pop Stop," she said. "What is it?"

"It's the greatest place to hang out on the Green." The Green is a huge park right in the middle of downtown Englewood. There are a lot of shops, offices, and restaurants around it. "They've got all kinds of different drinks and great food. Just about everyone goes there."

Heather didn't respond right away. "I'm not sure my mom will let me," she said. "She doesn't really like me to go to hangouts."

I couldn't imagine that anyone would not be allowed to go to the Pop Stop with friends. Rosie and I had been going there by ourselves for years. "It's just a regular restaurant. And the owners are always there. They make sure things don't get rowdy. I'll introduce you to them."

"Hold on a second," Heather said, then dropped the phone. I heard mumbling in the background, but I couldn't tell what anyone was saying.

A minute later Heather was back on the phone. "My mom said I could go...but would it be okay if you came over here to get me? She wants to meet you and Rosie first."

I wasn't sure how Rosie would feel about this, but I agreed anyway. "We'll be there at one o'clock. Oh, I almost forgot—can you get one of those pictures of Donny Davenport? I want to surprise Rosie." She agreed, and we said good-bye.

On Saturday afternoon Rosie looked great in her blue blouse and flowing multicolored miniskirt. I could always tell what kind of a mood Rosie was in from the way she dressed— the more colors, the happier.

"Those earrings are great," I said, referring to the silver dangles hanging from Rosie's earlobes. "What did you promise Anne you'd do to get her to lend them to you?"

"Hey, how'd you guess? I just have to take out the garbage for a week." Rosie made a face, then glanced at her watch. "Anyway, we'd better get going. I don't want to be late."

"On the way we need to make a stop," I mentioned casually.

"Where?" Rosie asked, without slowing down.

"Heather's house."

Rosie stopped dead in her tracks. "You invited her? I thought *we* were going together."

"Heather's never been to the Pop Stop. It'll be fun for her to see where everyone hangs out."

"That's why I don't want her there," she said, planting her fists on her hips.

"What are you talking about?"

"I just don't think she should come to the Pop Stop with us. *Everyone* will be there, and the popular kids don't like her."

"That's just because they don't know her. Besides, I've already invited her." My voice was shaking a little, and I swallowed hard to make the lump in my throat disappear. "I can't tell her I changed my mind."

Rosie put her hand to her chin. Then she looked up, her eyes brightening. "Maybe we could just tell her that in all of the excitement we forgot to get her."

"I'm not going to lie to her!"

"Then you'll have to figure out something, because I'm not going to the Pop Stop with Heather. She could really hurt our chances of becoming popular because she's...you know...nerdy."

"She's not nerdy. And if you'd just spend some time with her you'd know that."

Rosie tossed her head back and crossed her arms. "If you ask me, you're spending way *too much* time with her."

"No more than you spend with Shannon."

"Amy, now that we're in junior high, we have a chance to be a part of the popular crowd. You're going to have to choose who you'd rather be friends with."

"That sounds like something Shannon would say!"

"Don't bring her into this. She hasn't done anything to you."

"Yes, she has. I keep trying to tell you, but you won't listen. Shannon doesn't like me."

"Which is it, Amy—me or Heather?" Rosie stood as still as a statue and waited for my response.

"You can't expect me to make a choice like that!" I told her. "It's not fair. If you don't want to be friends anymore, just say so."

Rosie didn't answer. Instead, she stormed back into her house.

I watched the front door slam. The awful feeling in my chest got worse. Rosie liked going to the Pop Stop even more than I did. I was certain she'd never just stay home when she could be there instead. When the door didn't open, I could feel the tears in my eyes.

I couldn't stand outside the Bantons' house any longer. I was already late picking up Heather. But as I walked to Plum Street I couldn't get my argument with Rosie out of my mind. In the past our disagreements had always been between us—how I was always late, what movie we wanted to see, whether we should ride our bikes or walk to the Green. Now it wasn't just Rosie against me. It was Rosie against Heather and me. And me against Shannon and her gang, which now included Rosie. *And* Shannon and her gang against Heather.

I picked up a rock and threw it as hard as I could. It landed on the street three houses in front of me, then bounced into a nearby yard. It was a record throw for me, but I was feeling too hurt to be happy.

Chapter 6

Please, please, please just give me one more chance. The music blared from the Pop Stop's video jukebox.

When Heather and I got there, the Pop Stop was already packed. It was a typical Saturday afternoon crowd. Kids had practically filled up the red, white, and blue tables in the seating area. There was a huge line at the long counter in the front of the restaurant.

The only thing missing was Rosie. It seemed odd to be at the Pop Stop without her.

"Amy, how's Whitman treatin' ya?" a voice behind me asked. The heavy Southern accent was unmistakable. It was Mr. McAllister. He and his wife own the Pop Stop.

"Fine," I lied.

Looking frenzied, Mrs. McAllister rushed over. "This is my friend Heather," I told the

McAllisters. "She just moved here, and she goes to Whitman too."

Mr. McAllister and Heather shook hands. Mrs. McAllister gave her an affectionate squeeze on the arm. "It's a pleasure to meet you, Heather. I hope you like Englewood." She pushed her gray-and-black bangs off her forehead, then grabbed her husband's arm. "Now we've got work to do."

"Have fun, girls," Mr. McAllister said as he followed his wife to the kitchen.

"Thanks," Heather and I said at the same time.

We stepped in line. I looked up at the big chalkboard above the counter and studied the list of drinks, each written in a different color. I really didn't need to look at the menu since I almost always ordered the same thing—an Orange Smoothie—but I liked to check just in case there was something new. Orange is my favorite drink, flavor, and color.

"What are you going to have?" I asked Heather after I'd decided to get my usual drink.

Heather barely glanced at the crowded chalkboard. "Just a root beer."

"You can't get a soda here."

"But that sign says, 'Root Beer.'" She pointed

at the old-time soda machine behind the counter.

"Well, I mean you *can* get a soda, but with all of these other great drinks, why would you? How about a Brown Cow? It's root beer, with a scoop of vanilla ice cream," I suggested.

"Sounds good. Moooove over, soda. I am about to try something new and different."

"Hey, where'd you learn to do such a good cow impression?"

Heather cocked her head in an exaggerated gesture. "I guess you didn't know that I'm a cow expert. I used to live on a farm."

"Really? That must have been great."

"It was. There was always someone—well, some*thing*—to talk to."

Kristen Pagano pushed her light brown hair behind her ears. She and Lucy Cruz had been sitting together at the table when Heather and I came in. Once we got our drinks, we sat down with them.

"You guys are so lucky you have Mr. Norris," Kristen told Heather and me. "Mrs. Patterson is so boring." We laughed as she shut her eyelids and pretended to fall asleep. I knew Kristen from Cunningham Park. Sometimes she acted like an airhead, but she was actually pretty smart.

"Maybe you could transfer to our class," Heather suggested.

"And leave *me*?" Lucy shouted as she grabbed Kristen dramatically. "No way!"

"Besides, the cute guys are in Mrs. Patterson's class," Kristen added, raising her eyebrows mischievously.

"I don't know about that. We've got Glen Benedict," Heather pointed out.

"Ooooh!" the rest of us groaned. In less than a week, Glen had flirted with just about every girl in every one of his classes—and even some who weren't in his classes.

"Rosie told me he almost set your science room on fire," Lucy said. "She must have been furious."

I shrugged. "I guess so."

"Speaking of Rosie...where is she?" Kristen asked.

I knew it wouldn't take long for someone to ask about my best friend. We went together like pancakes and maple syrup. And nearly everyone at the Pop Stop knew that.

"She had something else she had to do," I said.

After that I completely tuned out what everyone was saying and tried to figure out if Rosie had really meant what she said about choosing between her and Heather.

"Hey, Amy," Heather's voice jolted me out of my thoughts. When I looked up, three sets of eyes were staring at me. "What were you thinking about?"

"Uh…oh…nothing. Just school."

"Well, you didn't have to go to another planet to do it," Heather joked. "That's what we were talking about too."

"Sorry."

Lucy sucked her chocolate milk shake up through her straw and swallowed. "Have you seen much of Englewood yet?" she asked Heather.

"Not really. I've just been trying to get used to school. I was pretty nervous about moving here. At my old school, we had only a hundred kids. There are more people at Whitman than in the whole town where I used to live!"

"Really?" Kristen asked.

Lucy rolled her eyes. "She's exaggerating, Kristen."

"Oh," Kristen said, sinking into her chair.

Lucy stood. "I hate to say it, but we'd better

get going. We've got to work on our science report."

"Can you believe it?" Kristen asked. "Mrs. Patterson is making us do a report over our first weekend."

"Maybe we could all go swimming in my pool before my parents close it up for the season," Lucy suggested.

Heather smiled and nodded. "That would be really fun."

"Good luck on your report!" I called as Lucy and Kristen headed out the door.

"They're really nice," Heather said. "Kristen's in my English and math classes, but I've never talked to her before."

"You're in advanced math and English? You must be a brain!" Only the twenty smartest kids got into those classes.

Heather's round face turned bright pink, and she looked down at her feet. "Not really."

"Don't be embarrassed about it. I think it's really cool. Believe me, I wish I did better in school."

Heather and I talked some more about our classes. We hadn't been alone very long when Shannon walked in with a couple of girls. Shannon stared right at me and Heather. She made her way past the counter, winding through the crowded tables. I could feel the knot in my stomach growing as Shannon stopped right next to me.

I picked up my Orange Smoothie and drank three huge gulps. Then I took a deep breath and prepared for a confrontation.

"Hi, Wendy," Shannon squealed, waving to a girl behind me.

I breathed a sigh of relief.

I turned around to face Heather, who was silently sipping her Brown Cow. "So tell me about the farm," I suggested, trying to get my mind off Shannon and Rosie.

Heather's face lit up with excitement. "Okay. Do you want to hear about the day the chickens flew the coop?"

"Sure."

"OK." Heather wiggled to the edge of her chair and put her arms on the table. "One day my mom and I were working in the fields. All of a sudden, we heard lots of clucking and horrible screeches. We raced over to the coop, where all the noise was coming from, and found out that somehow our Irish setter had gotten inside and had let all the chickens out."

"Oh, no! What did you do?"

"We started chasing them. As soon as Mom or I got close to a chicken, though, it would flap its wings and take off. Chickens can't fly very high or very far. But if you're small like me, they look as if they're headed right for your face. It can be pretty scary."

"Oh, my gosh—that's awful!"

"Actually, it was pretty funny. There were birds and people running around, and chicken feathers flying in all directions. When chasing them didn't work Mom decided to use chicken psychology. She stuck her elbows out like wings, moved her head back and forth, and clucked." Heather demonstrated and giggled.

"Did it work?" I asked.

"No. The chickens ran even farther away."

"Did you ever get them back in the coop?"

"When we finally gave up and went inside for dinner, so did they."

"It must be so different living in Englewood," I said to Heather when we both stopped laughing. "Are you glad you moved?"

Heather frowned and looked down at the table.

"Oh, I guess you didn't really want to move, did you? Sorry, I didn't mean to be nosy."

"It's okay," she said, swallowing hard. "A year

ago, my father died in a car crash."

I didn't know what to say. I'd never known anyone my age whose parent had died. I couldn't imagine not having both my mother and father around.

"Mom tried to keep the farm going after that—more for Daddy than for herself," Heather said solemnly, then she smiled and looked up at me. "But she's a better writer than farmer. It was hard for her to do both. I was really glad for Mom when the *Englewood Tribune* offered her the job." She scrunched up her small nose. "And I kind of wanted to get away from all of the memories of Daddy," she continued, twisting her hands in her lap.

"Well, I'm happy you moved here."

"Me too," she said. "The Pop Stop's really cool. Can you give me a tour of the rest of Englewood?"

"Sure! We can ride our bikes around tomorrow."

"Good. I finished all my homework last night. I don't have anything else to do." Heather picked up her empty cup. "I'm going to get another Brown Cow. Do you want anything?"

"No, thanks. I still have some left." Heather got up and went to stand in line.

As I waited for Heather to return, I sipped my drink and thought about her stories. But my good mood melted and my whole body froze when Rosie suddenly appeared in the Pop Stop doorway. When she spotted me, a huge smile spread across her face.

I smiled back. She walked between the crowded tables toward mine, then stopped next to me! Up close I could see that her eyes were red, as if she'd been crying.

"Amy, you came alone!" Rosie said.

Before I could explain, Shannon's voice cut in. "Rosie, I thought you'd never get here!"

Rosie looked at Shannon, then back at me.

"Hey, little sister," Anne called from behind the counter. Anne worked at the Pop Stop part-time. "I was wondering where you were." Rosie looked at her sister, then noticed Heather waiting in line at the counter.

Rosie's body stiffened, then she turned and walked—over to Shannon's table!

My stomach dropped to my feet. Our friendship was definitely over.

That evening, when I was in my bedroom, doing sit-ups to get in shape for track tryouts, I thought a lot about what a great afternoon I had

had with Heather. So why did I feel so crummy? I stopped exercising and wrapped my arms around my knees.

The reason was all around my room: Rosie.

My souvenir T-shirt from our trip to Washington, D.C., was lying in a heap on the floor in front of me. All of the stuffed animals she'd ever given me lined the shelf over my desk. Most painful of all was the picture of Rosie and me sitting on the beach, building a sandcastle. It was the best vacation ever. Mom and Dad had just gotten their divorce finalized, but my trip with the Bantons made me feel a million miles away from all the trouble back home. This time I couldn't just run over to the Bantons' to tell Rosie my problems. Rosie was my problem.

I pulled my diary out of my secret hiding place in the shoebox under my bed and began putting my thoughts on the page.

Dear Diary,
   Rosie and I had a huge fight today. We've had fights before, but this time it's different. Before, neither of us said we didn't want to be friends anymore. Maybe I shouldn't even care, because it seems that Rosie's really changing. She never used to act

so mean to people. I can't figure out what's going on with her. It's as if she thinks that just because we're in junior high school, we have to start acting phony and stupid.

One thing's for sure — I would never have dropped Rosie the way she dropped me. I thought that we were best friends forever. I guess I was wrong.

                      — I've lost my best friend, Amy

Chapter 7

"Come on, Heather!" I shouted as we pedaled away from the Dogwood Mall on Sunday.

"Can't...we...slow down...a little?" Heather panted. I squeezed the brakes on my silver ten-speed. "Sorry. I forgot you were used to riding horses, not bikes. I just want to make sure I show you everything." I slowed down the pace.

"I can't believe how huge that mall was!" Heather said for the fiftieth time.

The Dogwood Mall is five stories tall. Heather and I must have ridden the big glass elevator in the center at least ten times. We played with some puppies at the pet store, bought a music box for her mom at Gifts for All Occasions, and got soft pretzels at Sam's Hot Dog Stand. We even tried on wigs at Sasha's Hair Emporium until the saleswoman made us leave.

Now we were on our way to the Community Center, where I planned to show Heather all the electronic games, pinball machines, board games, and pool tables.

"I bet you thought I didn't even know what a video game was," she joked after her third victory on Sorcerer.

"Well, I have to admit I didn't think you had much of a chance to play them on the farm."

"What should we do now?" Heather shouted above the dinging machines and noisy kids around us.

"Let's get some ice cream and hang out on the Green."

As we pulled up on our bikes I spotted Simon playing Frisbee with his friends Mario Gomes and Chris Fisher. Simon waved and yelled, "Why didn't you get me any ice cream?"

"Guess who that is," I groaned under my breath, licking my scoop of orange sherbet to torment Simon. "My brother."

"He seems okay," Heather said. I rolled my eyes at her. Suddenly Heather's mouth flew open. "Look out!" she shouted. I looked up just in time to see the Frisbee knock my little brother on the back of the head. Heather and I laughed when Simon jokingly clutched his head and staggered across the grass.

We sat on a bench and watched the action in the park while we finished our cones. Nearby Aaron Greenberg and two other guys who went to Whitman, Josh Lefkowitz and Peter Martin, passed a soccer ball around with their feet. A few kids skated up and down the sidewalk in front of us on Rollerblades.

"Hey, you're going out for the track team, aren't you?" a voice beside me said. I recognized the speaker from the first day in the cafeteria—the blond guy who'd given Karen Patel his lunch.

"Yeah. How'd you know?"

"I've seen you practicing with Miss Keller. I'm going out for the team too." A warm smile spread across his face. "I'm Jake Meadows."

"Hi, I'm Amy," was all I could think to say.

"You don't have a thing to worry about. You'll definitely make the team."

My heart raced at the compliment. "Thanks." My face felt hot. "Well, we've got to get going." Just then, Shannon came up behind Jake and grabbed his hand. That could mean only one thing: Jake was Shannon's boyfriend! How could such a nice guy be dating such a snobby girl?

"We've got to meet Wendy, Trisha, and *Rosie* at the Pop Stop," Shannon told her boyfriend. I wasn't sure that she had seen me until I heard her emphasize Rosie's name.

"Shannon, do you know Amy?" Jake asked her. "She's in seventh grade too."

"Hi, Amy. I didn't see you." Shannon smiled sweetly. "We're in the same social studies class," she explained to Jake. She tugged on his arm. "Come on. We have to go."

"I'll see you at the track," Jake said, walking away.

Heather stood up beside me. "I didn't know you and Shannon were friends," she said, then put the final bite of ice cream cone into her mouth.

I shook my head. "We're not. Something very weird is going on."

My wet tennis shoes squished as I trudged down the hall Wednesday morning. As I walked all the way to school in the rain, they'd gone from white and stiff to dirty and flexible.

"I just bought those for you," my mother had complained as I was walking out the door that morning.

"That's why I'm wearing them. They're too new."

It was pretty uncomfortable—and loud—walking around in shoes that squished water every time I took a step. But once they dried it would be worth it.

There was just one thing wrecking my mood. I really missed Rosie. Walking to school with her on rainy days had always been a lot of fun. I searched for the deepest puddles to wade through, while Rosie avoided them completely and jokingly complained when I accidentally splashed her.

It wasn't just a coincidence that I never ran into Rosie on the way to school anymore. I had been watching from my bedroom window every morning to see her leave.

Heather was waiting for me when I got to my locker. All week she had been meeting me there before first period. Now that I didn't have anyone to walk to school with, it made me feel good to see her first thing. Since her mother still drove her to school every morning, she was completely dry.

"What's this?" I asked, pulling a folded piece of paper out of the slots in my locker.

"It was there when I got here," Heather explained.

I unfolded the paper. "It's a note—from Glen Benedict."

"Why did he write you a note? He sits next to you in science." When I'd gotten to sixth period on Monday, instead of Rosie I had found Glen sitting at our table. At first I'd been a little relieved that I didn't have to face Rosie. After four days, though, I was getting kind of tired of Glen's staring at me, then pretending he wasn't doing anything when I looked over at him.

I quickly read Glen's messy handwriting. "He likes me. *Really* likes me."

"You mean, as in *boyfriend* likes you?"

I nodded.

"Poor Amy. What's the note say?"

"'Dear Amy,'" I read. "'You are the prettiest girl I know. Will you go out with me? Check one—yes, no, maybe.' What am I going to do?"

"Why don't you just tell him you don't like him?" Heather suggested.

"I can't do that. It might hurt his feelings."

"Yeah, Glen's pretty goofy, but he's nice. You don't want to be mean." Heather tilted her head to one side and looked ahead at nothing in particular. "I know—tell him your parents won't let you go out with anyone yet."

"But what if I ever want to go out with someone else? If I do, Glen will know I lied. Maybe I just won't do anything. He probably stuck the same note in fifty girls' lockers anyway. He'll be so busy getting answers from everyone else, I bet he won't even notice that I didn't say anything."

"For your sake, I hope you're right."

I shoved my backpack in my locker. "I'm sure I am."

Heather and I pushed our way through a group of boys crowding the hall. "I almost forgot to ask you," Heather told me. "My mom said it was okay for you spend a night at my house this weekend if you want."

"Great! I have to check with my parents, but I'm sure they'll say yes."

"Perfect. How about Friday?" Heather's face became serious. "I have to warn you, though. My mom will probably hang out with us a lot. She's kind of overprotective."

"Is that because your father died?"

"That's when it started. But she's also pretty nervous about me being in a big town." Heather turned into her English classroom. "Well, I'll see you at lunch."

I walked toward the gym. Except for a few slumber parties with a bunch of other girls there, I had never spent the night at anyone's house but Rosie's. For me, Heather's invitation was a really big deal.

Up ahead, I could see a group of girls huddled around Shannon Sommer. Of course, Rosie was there too. I considered turning around and taking another route to the gym.

Rosie didn't seem to see me, though, so I decided to take a chance and continued walking toward the group.

Actually, I wasn't sure if I wanted Rosie to notice me or not. Maybe she missed me as much as I missed her. If she did, this could be our chance for a big reunion.

As I got closer I could hear Shannon's obnoxious voice above all of the other noise in the hall. "Well, I hope she doesn't think she's special. Jake is nice to everybody." Shannon's friends nodded sympathetically.

"At least you don't have to worry about her stealing him away," Wendy consoled Shannon. All the other girls laughed uproariously at the thought—all except Rosie. She bit her lip and shifted nervously from one foot to the other. They were all so busy gossiping that they didn't notice me approaching.

I wonder who they're picking on today, I thought, pretending to look at the lockers on the other side of the hall.

"I just feel sorry for you, Rosie," Shannon continued loudly. "You have to live next door to her."

They're talking about me! And I knew why. The day before, I had stayed after school to run some laps on the track. Toward the end of the workout, Jake had run around the track a couple times with me to help me pace myself. Of course, Shannon showed up just as we were finishing.

All she said was, "Good luck at tryouts next week." But now I knew she had been completely fake just because Jake was there.

I slowed down, trying to hear what else the stuck-up girls had to say about me.

"Don't worry," a girl named Kara said. "Jake has lots of friends who are girls."

Shannon crossed her arms angrily. "I just think he should choose them more carefully."

"You're not going to stop dating the cutest guy in school just because of Amy Leonard, are you, Shannon?" Wendy asked, giggling slyly.

"Of course not. After all, he's dating me, not her."

I couldn't believe I had been getting to Shannon without even trying. She really must have been upset by the fact that Jake was paying attention to me.

My thoughts shifted from Shannon to Rosie. Even though she'd had an opportunity, Rosie hadn't joined in the Amy-bashing. Instead, she'd just continued to look at the ground awkwardly.

I wish I knew what she's thinking. I turned the corner and headed toward the gym.

After I'd changed into my gym clothes I sat on the bench and waited for Rosie to walk through the locker room doors.

Where can she be? I wondered. I couldn t stay much longer or I'd be late for class. Most of the other girls were already lined up in their squads when I'd passed through the gym.

As I reached down to pull up my socks, Rosie rushed into the room and sped to her locker. I took a deep breath, stood up, and headed toward her.

"You'd better hurry or you'll be late," I said, standing behind her as she opened her locker.

Rosie looked at me expressionless. "Uh huh."

"It's a joke—get it? I'm usually the one who's late."

Rosie looked at me without smiling. "I get it."

"Why won't you talk to me anymore?"

Rosie didn't answer. She pulled her gym clothes out of her locker.

"Why can't we be friends?" I asked.

Rosie pulled her yellow tank top off over her head. "You wouldn't understand."

"No, I don't understand. I miss you, and I think you miss me, but you're being really weird about this."

"Why would you miss me? You've got other friends. And so do I." She continued dressing without looking at me.

"We've always had other friends. But we're *best* friends." Above us, the late bell rang out from the wall.

"You're right," Rosie said, slamming her locker. "We're late." She rushed out of the locker room.

I couldn't believe it. For four years, Rosie

had been my best friend in the world. Now we could barely even have a conversation. Things were definitely going from bad to worse.

Dear Diary,

Since I can't even get Rosie to talk to me, I'm never going to find out what's going on. How did things ever get so messed up between us? This isn't like the little fights we've had. I've never felt so horrible before.

                    – Confused, Amy

P.S. Today Glen gave me a box of chocolate candy in science. Yuck! I told him I'm allergic to chocolate and gave it back.

Chapter 8

"Mom! If you don't quit stealing cookie dough, there won't be anything left to bake," Heather scolded her mother.

Ms. Cohen licked her finger, then sat back down at the kitchen table. "All right," she said, sighing dramatically. "I'll just sit here all alone with nothing to do."

Heather continued slicing cookies from her roll of dough. "Good." She leaned toward me and said, "She's never been very good at laying a guilt trip on me."

I giggled. Heather and her mother had been teasing each other ever since I arrived for the sleepover. In a lot of ways, they were more like sisters than mother and daughter—except I knew that as much as Ms. Cohen might like being with Heather and her friends, the real reason she hung around was to make sure we didn't get into trouble...on purpose or accidentally.

I didn't mind having Ms. Cohen around, though. I'd met her before, when Heather and I went to the Pop Stop on Saturday, but that was just to say "hi." This was my first real chance to find out what she was like.

From what Heather had told me, I half expected Ms. Cohen to be like the widows in the old movies my dad watched, with her hair pulled back tight, a grim expression, and a black dress. Instead, she had long wavy red hair in a loose braid, and she was wearing yellow leggings and a shirt with huge daisies. Her features were long and thin, but in a dramatic, not depressed, way.

With Ms. Cohen in such a good mood, this was the perfect time to ask the big question. I turned to Heather and silently mouthed, "Should we ask her?"

Heather nodded enthusiastically. "Now's as good a time as any."

"For what?" Ms. Cohen asked suspiciously.

I cleared my throat. "Heather and I were wondering if she could start walking to school with me."

"Oh, I don't know whether—"

"Mom, lots of kids do it. Amy's parents let her walk to and from school every day."

"But Amy lives closer to school than you do," her mother explained.

"Just two blocks," I cut in. "That's practically nothing."

"Well…okay," Ms. Cohen said. "But I'll still pick you up when you have to stay late for band practice."

"Yea!" we shouted in unison. Heather and I gave each other a high-five, and Heather did a little dance around the kitchen. When her dance was over, she hugged her mother. "You are the most wonderful, spectacular, fabulous—"

"I know, I know. Now hurry up and put those cookies in the oven before I eat them all raw."

We quickly sliced the remaining dough and slid the cookie trays into the hot oven.

Heather made a motion for me to follow her out of the kitchen. "Come on," she said. "I'll introduce you to my pets. Mom, will you please take the cookies out when they're ready?"

"You bet!"

As we walked into the family room, we were greeted by Heather's Pekingese, her tongue hanging out of the side of her mouth and a tiny pink bow on her head. She flopped onto her back and put her paws in the air.

"You've already met Rexi," Heather said.

I bent over to scratch the dog's stomach. When I had arrived at the Cohens' that evening, Heather was trying to teach Rexi how to fetch a stick and bring it back to her. Instead, Rexi kept hiding the sticks behind the bushes.

Heather tapped on the side of a glass tank. "That's Ned on the exercise wheel." A fuzzy yellow ball of fur kept running inside what looked like a miniature Ferris wheel. "He's a golden hamster."

I pointed to the other hamster, who had a protruding belly and was lying on a pile of wood chips in the corner. "What's wrong with him?"

"That's Hedda. She's a girl, and she's going to have babies soon. You can have one if you want."

"Cool." I looked into the next cage. "Ugh! What is that?"

Heather lifted the lid and pulled out a white rat. "This is Ben."

She put the rat on her shoulder and held her arm straight out in front of her. Ben ran to her fingertips. "A lot of people think rats are dirty animals, but they're not. And Ben likes affection just as much as Rexi does." At the mention of her name, Rexi charged over to us and flipped upside down. "Well, maybe not that much. But rats are really smart."

A prickly feeling spread over my back as Ben raced back up Heather's arm and scurried onto her head. "Okay, I believe you. But if Ben has any babies, I don't think I want one."

Next I met Boa the garter snake and Flopsy the lop-eared rabbit. The last stop was a huge fish tank. Heather shook a can of food over the top. A rush of colors moved through the water as the fish raced to get their dinner. One blue fish stayed behind and stared through the glass, opening and closing his mouth and wiggling his fins, which looked like ears.

"His name is Shark," Heather explained, making a face at him. "I'm thinking about changing it to Glen, though, since he and Glen Benedict look so much alike."

"Don't remind me about Glen," I said. "Today he asked me to go to the Virginia State Fair with him. I told him I couldn't go because I was spending the night over here. I owe you big-time."

Heather giggled, then her face got serious. "Why did Rosie switch seats with Glen anyway? I thought you and she were friends."

"*Were* is right. She's changed a lot since we started at Whitman."

"How could she change so much in two weeks?"

I shrugged. "She really wants to be part of the popular crowd. And it looks as if she's getting what she wants."

"I bet you really miss her," Heather said sympathetically. She waited for my response, but I didn't say anything. I really liked Heather and knew I could trust her, but I wasn't quite ready to share the important stuff.

"Did I have anything to do with your fight with Rosie?" Heather asked. "I noticed that she didn't sit with us at the Pop Stop on Saturday."

"Like I said, Rosie's changed a lot." Neither of us spoke for a few minutes after that.

"Hey, would you play something on your sax?" I asked, looking for something to take our minds off Rosie.

"Well, I'm a little out of practice."

"Come on, Heather. Just play anything."

I followed her down the hall into her bedroom. She pulled the sax out of its case, blew into the instrument a few times, then played a jazzy piece.

"Man, that was great!" I said when Heather had finished. "I usually don't even like music unless it's got words. What was that called?"

Heather caught her breath. "'In a Sentimental Mood.' It has words. It's just kind of hard to sing with an instrument in your mouth. I played it in the music competition at my school last year."

"Did you win?"

Heather blushed and looked at the ground. "Well, yeah."

Just then Ms. Cohen's voice called, "Come on, girls! Pizza's here."

"All right!" I yelled, heading for the door. "Let's pig out!"

Ms. Cohen pulled herself off the couch and ejected the tape from the VCR. "That deserved an Academy Award."

"You said that about the other movie, too,"

Heather reminded her, then turned to me. "If it makes her cry, she thinks it deserves an award."

"Everyone's a critic." Heather's mother threw a wad of tissues at her. "I'm going to get ready for bed, and you girls should think about doing the same." She raised her hand in the air, flicked her wrist dramatically, and strutted out of the room.

I laughed and shook my head. I had never met a parent as silly as Ms. Cohen. She had even let us stay up until nearly one o'clock in the morning!

"Your mom's so cool," I told Heather, as if she didn't already know.

"Yeah, I guess she is pretty cool." She pushed her glasses up on her nose. "You would have liked Dad, too."

"What was he like?"

Heather stared up at the ceiling. "Every Saturday he'd take me to a flea market or a garage sale and buy me a gift. Mom would scream when we got back because it was always something old and worthless—like a ceramic sculpture without a head or a broken-down record player. He said he'd fix everything when he got around to it."

Heather turned to me as though she'd just remembered that I was in the room. "It's easier here," she said. "There aren't so many memories. The farm really was his home."

Listening to Heather talk about her father made me realize that we had a lot in common. "I miss having my dad home all the time too."

"Where is he?"

"He lives in Williamston. My parents are divorced."

"Who answered the phone when I called yesterday?"

"That was Paul, my stepfather. Mom married him two years ago. Their last name is Spinosa."

"Do you like him?"

"Oh, yeah. Paul's great." Heather raised her left eyebrow at me. "Well, I didn't think so at first. I swore I'd never be happy unless my parents got back together."

"You must have been really miserable."

"Probably not half as miserable as I was making my mother and father. Even though they told me a million times that they just couldn't live together, I was convinced I would change their minds."

"What changed *your* mind?"

"Well, I kind of got it through my skull when

both of them remarried—first Mom and Paul, then Dad and Molly last year. Molly has a four-year-old daughter named Emily Erickson."

"You sure have a lot of different names in your family."

"Tell me about it. Actually, my dad's trying to adopt Emily so that she'll be a Leonard too, but it's not final yet."

Ms. Cohen peeked her head into the room. "Okay, chatterboxes. You'd better get some sleep or you'll be zombies in the morning. I don't need any monsters at the breakfast table." She blew Heather a kiss.

"OK, Mom," Heather called out. "Good night."

"Good night," I echoed.

As I tried to fall asleep I thought about how much fun I was having at Heather's. Then my mind wandered to what it used to be like at my sleepovers with Rosie. She already knew all about the divorce. She had even been at both of the weddings. There was no doubt about it— Rosie knew me better than anyone else did.

But as much as I missed Rosie, it was fun hanging out with Heather and finding out all kinds of stuff about her.

Maybe new friends are just as good as old ones.

"Thanks for letting me sleep over, Ms. Cohen," I said the next morning, swinging my backpack over my shoulders and picking up my sleeping bag. "I had a really good time."

Ms. Cohen smiled. "I'm glad you could come."

"I'll call you tomorrow," Heather said.

I walked out of the Cohens' house and down the two blocks to mine. I was thinking so hard about all the new stuff I'd learned about Heather's family that I almost didn't notice Rosie standing in her front yard.

She was wearing white shorts, a white tank top, and a turquoise vest—not the kind of outfit she'd wear to clean up the yard or wash Anne's car. In fact, it didn't look as if she was doing anything but standing there watching me!

I couldn't take my eyes off her. Her dark eyes were droopy, which made her whole face look sad.

Suddenly my heart skipped a beat. *Maybe Rosie wants to be friends again*, I thought. *Maybe she's just afraid to make the first move after what happened in the locker room the other day.*

I stopped halfway across my front yard. "Hi," I said. My heart was trying to leap out of my chest.

Rosie opened her mouth to speak, then stopped when she saw the orange sleeping bag in my hand.

Before I could say anything else, she turned and raced into her house.

Dear Diary,

I don't know what to do. I keep hoping Rosie's still my best friend, because she's been my friend for four years. But I also want Heather to be my best friend, because she's so funny and nice. I don't think she can be my best friend, though, unless I tell her all of the horrible stuff that's going on with Rosie. But it might hurt her feelings if I tell her that she's one of the reasons we had a fight.

Actually, that's not the whole truth. I also don't feel right talking about Rosie behind her back. I guess deep down I still want to be friends. Pretty stupid, huh? Rosie's a real member of Shannon's group

now. Shannon was even wearing one of
Rosie's new sweaters on Friday. Sometimes I
wish I could forget all about Rosie Banton!
                                    -S.O.S., Amy

"Amy, there's someone here to see you," Paul called up to my bedroom later that afternoon.

I can't believe it! I thought. Rosie actually changed her mind.

"Coming!" I shouted. I closed the diary, slid it under my bed, and ran downstairs.

But instead of Rosie, a human-size green stuffed rabbit was standing by the front door. "Hi, Amy!" the rabbit said without moving its lips.

Then Glen Benedict peeked out from behind the stuffed animal. "Sorry you couldn't come to the fair. I won this for you at the basketball toss."

"I didn't know you played basketball."

Glen blushed. "I don't. But I just kept playing until I got them all in."

My stomach dropped. It was clear that Glen

liked me even more than I'd realized.

"Um…I have to tell you something," I began. "I don't really—"

"Who wants lemonade?" Paul shouted from the kitchen.

"I do," Glen answered quickly. "I had to carry this all the way over here," he told me. Then he handed me the giant rabbit.

I propped up my present on the living room couch and walked into the kitchen, where Glen was already sitting down at the table with a superlarge glass of lemonade in front of him. Glen would be here all afternoon if he planned to finish that entire glass.

Paul set one in front of me, too. "I'll leave you guys alone. If you want more lemonade, there's a pitcherful in the refrigerator."

"Thanks," I said, frowning.

Glen watched me sip my lemonade, then picked up his glass and gulped the entire thing. *Good*, I thought, *now he can go home*.

"Could I have some more?" he asked.

"Sure." I dragged myself over to the refrigerator and pulled the door open.

Glen looked around our big kitchen. "Is your mother here?"

"No, she had to work today."

"That's too bad. I'd like to meet her some-time."

I sat down at the table across from Glen and gave him my most serious look. "It was really nice of you to come here and bring me the rabbit and everything, but—"

A loud slam interrupted me. "Hey, where'd the cool rabbit come from?" Simon asked from the foyer.

As my little brother came into the kitchen, Glen looked up from the table. "I gave it to Amy," he said.

"What'd you do that for? You should have kept it."

"I won it for *her*."

"*Oh*, I get it," Simon said, grinning obnoxiously. He walked over to the refrigerator and pulled out a bowl of tuna salad.

"Come on, Glen," I said. "Let's go outside." If I was ever going to make Glen understand that I didn't like him the way he liked me, I needed to have some privacy.

"Oh, I'm sorry. Did you guys want to be *alone*?" Simon asked. I shot him a nasty look and led Glen to the front porch.

Glen sat down on the front steps, so I kept

standing. "Um, Glen, why did you ask me to the fair and bring me the rabbit? I thought you liked a lot of other girls."

Glen shrugged. "None of them are as nice to me as you are."

"Maybe that's because you're such a flirt. Sometimes girls don't like that."

"Don't worry. Now that you're my girlfriend I won't do that anymore."

"Hey, Amy and Glen," a voice called from the street. Peter Martin had parked his black dirt bike on the side of the road in front of my house.

Oh, no—not someone from school! I thought as Peter stared at us.

Just when I thought I was as miserable as I possibly could be, Aaron Greenberg rode up behind him. He has the biggest mouth in the entire seventh grade.

"We're going to the Community Center game room," Aaron explained. "Want to come?"

"No, thanks," I said, relieved that he hadn't teased us about being together.

"I'll come," Glen said, jumping off the step. "I'll see you later, Amy." He ran across my front yard.

What a relief! I was sorry I had been such a wimp about telling Glen I didn't want to be his girlfriend. But I was happy that he was gone— until I walked into the house and saw the huge green bunny grinning at me.

"Come on, Amy," my father encouraged me over the clinking of barbells around us. "Two weeks ago, this was easy for you." I had called Dad and asked him to come with me to the Community Center weight room. I thought it might take my mind off my problems. Plus, I needed to get serious about track tryouts, which were on Wednesday.

Taking a deep breath, I tried again to push the heavy barbell away from my chest. "It's...too...heavy," I grunted, unable to make it budge.

Dad's shaggy blond hair hung in his eyes as he leaned over the bench from his spotting position. "I'll take some of this weight off for you," he offered. He picked up the bar with one hand.

Slowly, I sat up on the edge of the bench and wiped the sweat off my forehead with a towel. "I guess Heather and I stayed up pretty late last night."

Dad slid two 5-pound weights off the bar. "Mmm hmm."

I couldn't dodge the truth. I was more than tired. My body ached, and I felt really weak. If I was getting sick, I was sure I could forget about making the track team.

The next morning wasn't any better. The aches still had control of my body.

I forced my eyelids open and looked at the clock on my nightstand. Eight fifty-two. Eight minutes to Sunday breakfast, which has been a family tradition ever since Mom married Paul.

I was glad it was Simon's week to help Mom. I flipped over and shut my eyes again, hoping to fall back to sleep.

The smell of waffles floated up the stairs to my bedroom. No one makes waffles like my mother. Actually, no one cooks as well as she does, but her waffles are my absolute favorite.

My muscles were telling me to stay in bed, but my stomach cried out for waffles. Of course, my stomach won.

I flung my off orange comforter and planted my feet on the floor, ready to race downstairs. But as I stood up I felt even worse.

Maybe a shower will help, I decided.

I dragged myself down the hall and into the bathroom. Still groggy, I pulled my football jersey over my head, then slipped off my underwear. As I reached over to turn on the water, I noticed a brownish red stain in my underwear. I blinked. *I'm not really awake yet*, I told myself. But when I opened my eyes, the mark was still there. I had gotten my period in the night!

I leaned over the sink, looked at myself in the mirror, and examined my reflection. I expected to see AMY GOT HER PERIOD written across my forehead, but I looked exactly the same as I had the day before.

There's no way anyone will know unless I tell them, I thought as I stepped into the shower. Getting your period is pretty personal—not like winning a tennis championship, where there's an announcement over the public address system and you get a trophy. This would have to be a secret victory.

Over the noise of the shower, I heard pounding on the door. I turned off the water. "Who is it?" I hardly needed to ask. My little brother has a unique way of making his presence obvious.

"Mom says that if you don't come down right now, breakfast will get cold."

"I'm coming." I grabbed my towel and wrapped it around my body.

"Okay, but if you're not downstairs in two minutes, I get to eat your waffles."

"Tell Mom I need her," I told Simon.

"Why?"

I gritted my teeth. "Because I said to."

While I waited for my mother, I opened the door to the vanity under the sink and reached for her maxi pads. This morning, I considered them as much mine as hers. Unfortunately, Mom and I had only one left.

After I dried myself, I hurried to my room to get dressed.

I pulled my underwear halfway up, then tore the paper strip off the napkin and stuck on the pad. Unfortunately, I didn't do a very good job. More of it was stuck to my leg than my underwear. The second time I did a little better.

Pretty good for a chestless tomboy, I thought, pulling my underwear up the rest of the way.

The sex-education films we'd seen in school had said that I wouldn't be able to tell I was even wearing a maxi pad. But the films lied. The pad felt huge between my legs. I decided that those films were definitely made by men who had no idea what it was like to get your period.

As I pulled on my blue jeans and Washington Bullets T-shirt, I thought about what getting my period meant. I knew my mom would say I was really growing up. But I wasn't too thrilled with the aches—or feeling as if I had a throw pillow between my legs.

My mother tapped lightly on my bedroom door. "Amy, is everything all right?"

I opened the door and waved my hand furiously to motion her inside. She stepped in and shut the door behind her. "Aren't you coming down for Sunday breakfast?" she asked. "Your waffles are stone-cold."

I couldn't wait to tell her my big news. I felt as if I was going to explode. "Guess what? I got my period!"

Mom clapped her hands together, then took a deep breath. "That's wonderful! Do you have any questions you want to ask me?"

"I hope not. I mean, I've been hearing and learning about it for the past three years. If I don't know it all by now, I'm in trouble!"

"You'd be surprised about how much you still have to learn," Mom said, blinking to hide the tears that I could see building up. "You're not a little girl anymore. You're a woman. If there's anything you want to discuss, you know you can come talk to me."

"Mom, I haven't been a little girl for a long time!" I twisted a strand of my wet, tangled hair. "I guess it did sort of surprise me, though. I don't even have anything else yet." I looked down at my flat, hipless body. In the sex education films, the girls had usually developed hips and breasts by the time they got their periods. If it weren't for my long hair, I could still pass for a boy.

"Some girls mature differently," my mother explained.

I couldn't help thinking about Rosie. She definitely looked like the girls in the films. She had been wearing a bra since fifth grade. I sat down on the edge of my bed and hung my head. "Yeah, I guess so."

"Sweetheart, what's wrong?" Mom sat down close to me, even though there was plenty of room on the edge of the bed.

"This is the biggest day of my life and I can't even tell Rosie." I couldn't hold back the tears that flowed down my face. "Rosie hates me, and she won't tell me why," I said, squeezing my mother tight.

She wrapped her arms around me. "I had a suspicion something was going on between you two."

"I've tried to make up twice, but she doesn't want to."

Mom raised her eyebrows and smiled slightly. "Sometimes things seem twice as bad when you're having your period. Besides, you and Rosie have gone through some really big changes lately. You haven't even had a chance to get used to your new school yet. I think Rosie will come around pretty soon."

"I hope so," I agreed halfheartedly, and wiped my eyes with the tail of my T-shirt.

Mom got up from the bed. "Did you find the maxi pads?"

I nodded. "I used your last one."

"We'll make a trip to the drugstore together after breakfast."

I jumped off the bed. "*I* have to go?"

"It's not as horrible as it sounds. Besides, you'll have to get used to it."

Standing reminded me about my various aches and pains. "Will I also get used to the cramps?"

"They'll go away. Some months you won't

even get them." She grabbed the doorknob.

"Why did I have to get them *this* month? Tryouts for the track team are on Wednesday."

"By Wednesday you'll forget you had them," she said, giving me a comforting look. "This isn't going to affect your athletic performance in any way." She sounded just like the sex ed films, and they'd already been wrong. "Why don't you come down to breakfast?"

"In a minute. There's something I have to do first."

After Mom shut the door, I pulled my diary out of its hiding place, grabbed a pen, and plopped down on the floor.

The waffles can wait! I thought.

Dear Diary,

I got my period! I'm not sure how I feel about it, though. I promised Rosie she'd be the first to know (after my mom). Do you have to keep a promise to your best friend if you're not even friends anymore?

Anyway, it's kind of stupid to think about, since now Rosie would probably just think I was a baby for making such a big deal out of it. Shannon probably got her period a long time ago.

The only way my life could get worse is if I don't make the track team.

Feeling funky, Amy

Chapter 10

As soon as the light turned green my mother hit the accelerator. She had insisted that we go to the drugstore right after breakfast, even though I had hoped to spend the rest of the morning training for track tryouts. I had taken an aspirin and my cramps were almost completely gone.

Together we had decided that junior-size tampons would probably be best for me, since I was really into sports, but I would also get maxi pads just in case.

"Do any of your friends have their periods yet?" Mom asked.

I shrugged. "I think Claudia does." When she had pulled her glove out of her gym bag one day at softball practice, some tampons fell out. I just pretended I didn't see them, and she hadn't said anything.

Heather and I hadn't covered the subject yet. If I really wanted to know, I could just ask her. Rosie was a different story. For all I knew, she had gotten hers in the past week. If she had, Shannon probably knew all about it—if Rosie had broken her promise to tell me first, that is.

Mom pulled the van into the Shop-a-Lot parking lot.

We entered the store and I followed my mom to the aisle we needed. Fortunately, no one was around except my mother, so I quickly grabbed a small box of tampons off the shelf.

"You'd better get one of these," she said, pointing to a box four times the size. "Otherwise you'll have to keep buying more every month. Besides, they're on sale."

I put back the small box and picked up the larger one, once again inspecting the aisle for spies.

My mother slid to the right and studied a box of maxi pads, the same kind she kept in the bathroom. "This brand is good. They're a little bigger than some of the others, but you won't have to worry about stains."

I quickly turned to her. "Just tell me which ones to get," I whispered. "You don't have to tell me *why*."

"Sorry," she said, smiling slightly. Then in a fake whisper, she added, "Get *these*." Unfortunately, I didn't have the same sense of humor. My face was getting hot from embarrassment, and I was sure that if I didn't get some fresh air in about thirty seconds, I would pass out.

"I've got to go outside."

"Oh, no, you don't. I've got my hands full." To emphasize her point, she showed me the makeup and paper towels she was carrying.

I let out a deep breath and reached for the box of maxi pads.

"Let's go," I said.

As we got closer to the front, though, I was relieved to discover that the cashier was female. I walked a little faster, happy to be nearing the homestretch.

I took one last look around. *Oh, no!* I exclaimed silently as the blood drained from my face. Glen Benedict was heading straight toward me!

"Hey, Amy," Glen's loud voice shouted behind me before I could hide. His skinny body galumphed toward me and my mother. "I thought that was you. I could hardly tell with that baseball cap. How ya doing?"

I was trapped!

"I'm okay, Glen," I said halfheartedly, as I tried to hide the boxes behind my back. It was like trying to hide King Kong behind a car. "But I'm in a big hurry," I added quickly.

Glen looked at my mother, and a goofy smile spread across his face. "Aren't you going to introduce me?"

"This is my mom. Mom, this is Glen Benedict. He sits next to me in science. Okay, I've got to go now," I said, and started to walk backward. One of the boxes started to slip out of my hand but I managed to pin it against my leg.

"It's very nice to meet you," Glen told my mother.

My mother had a huge grin across her face. "It's nice to meet you, too. That was very nice of you to win the rabbit for Amy."

Glen looked at me with his big lovesick eyes. All of a sudden, the box of maxi pads slipped out of my hand and made a loud *clunk* as it hit the floor.

Glen reached down to pick up the package, and my heart stopped beating. I bent over to grab the box before he could.

When his body froze, I knew it was too late. Without standing up completely, he backed away, nearly tripping over his long feet.

"Uh...uh..." he stammered, swallowing ha
"I'd better go." He spun around and rushed o
the drugstore exit.

I had to laugh. Glen was even more freake
out than I was. And I was pretty sure he
wouldn't be bugging me anymore with candy
or giant rabbits.

"Why do they look so weird?" I asked Heather,
peering in at the baby hamsters nuzzling up to
their mother. After my mom and I had gotten
back from the Shop-a-Lot, Heather had called
to tell me to come over right away because she
had a surprise for me. I was shocked to see the
newborn hamsters. Instead of being cute and
yellow and fuzzy, like Hedda and Ned, they
were tiny pale pink lumps.

"They're only a couple of hours old. When I
called you, there were only three babies. Now
there are six."

"Wow! Six babies at once! No wonder
Hedda looks so tired."

"The babies won't be able to leave her for a
little while, but you can have one if you want
when they're old enough. Hamsters are pretty
easy. I'll give you all of our old books and help
you out if you need it."

"I have to come up with a name. What are you going to name the other ones?"

"That's easy. Ted, Fred, Red, Ed, and..."

"How about Jed?" Ms. Cohen suggested as she carried a hamster water bottle into the room. When she slid it onto the inside wall of the cage, Ned rushed over to get a drink.

Heather's face brightened. "Excellent!"

"Those are all boy's names. What if they're girls?"

"In that case," Heather said, "Tedda, Fredda, Redda, Edda, and Jedda." Ms. Cohen nodded in agreement, as if those were the most normal names in the world.

"Well, the name I've picked isn't going to rhyme," I said. "Martina—or Martin if it's a boy."

"Why?" Heather asked.

"For Martina Navratilova, the best tennis player ever."

"Now that that's taken care of, we'd better leave the new family alone," Ms. Cohen suggested. "If you need me, I'll be working in my office."

When her mother was gone, Heather turned and looked at me slyly. "Mom went shopping today. Let's raid the kitchen."

"I'm right behind you!"

We brought nacho chips, chocolate-covered marshmallow cookies, cupcakes, and sodas to the table.

"Does your mother always buy you stuff like this?" I asked.

"Doesn't yours?"

"No way. At my last birthday party, we had carrot sticks, unsalted nuts, and bagel chips."

"That's sounds pretty healthy."

"And boring," I added, ripping open the cookies.

Heather poured us each a soda, then sat down at the table. "Have you gotten any more love letters from Glen?"

I told her all about the giant green rabbit and how I'd been humiliated when Peter and Aaron rode up.

"At least you *tried* to tell him the truth. It's not your fault everybody kept butting in."

"It turns out I didn't need to tell him after all." As soon as I'd said it, I realized my mistake. I didn't know how to tell Heather about getting rid of Glen without also telling her about getting my period.

"You didn't?"

"Um…I mean…I just have a feeling he doesn't like me anymore."

"Is he mad at you?"

"Not exactly."

"Oh," Heather said quietly.

The sad look on Heather's face made me feel awful. Why was I still worried about keeping my promise to Rosie? I was dreaming if I thought we'd ever be friends again.

I wished I could explain it all to Heather, but I didn't understand it myself.

Dear Diary,

Heather knows I'm keeping something from her. I've got all this stuff that I want to tell her, but I feel as if I can't. The problem is that even though Rosie gave up on me a long time ago, I can't give up on our friendship. It just wouldn't seem right to confide in Heather, when I'd promised Rosie I would tell her first. Even though Heather's great, she can't replace my best friend of four years—not yet anyway.

— Amy the crummy friend

Chapter 11

"Let's do those calf stretches that Miss Keller showed us yesterday," Sherry Lane suggested. She had gone to Englewood Elementary. I'd seen her around, at the Pop Stop and on the Green, but we'd never talked until track practice.

"Good idea," I agreed, sitting down on the grass beside her.

I appreciated any distraction that would help me get my mind off my tryout—and Shannon Sommer. She and Wendy were sitting in the bleachers across from us, waiting to watch Jake compete. Unlike the other fans and spectators, Shannon kept shooting me dirty looks.

In a way, I was actually sorry that Rosie wasn't with her new friends in the stands. She had always cheered for me at big sports events like this, and it seemed strange without her.

"We're next," Sherry said excitedly, pointing to the final group of eighth-grade boys lining up.

The muscles in my legs tightened, and my stomach felt as if I'd just gone down a major hill on a roller coaster. "Already?"

"A few minutes ago you were complaining that it was taking too long," Claudia reminded me.

"I guess I'm a little nervous." My cramps had disappeared on Sunday morning, so after I got back from Heather's I had spent the rest of that day—and Monday and Tuesday—training. Still, something just wasn't right.

I turned to watch the boys lining up. Jake Meadows bounced in his lane, shaking his arms and legs. None of the other racers looked as calm and confident as he did.

The starter gun went off, and Jake sprinted out front immediately. His body moved smoothly around the track. He never even looked to see how close the other runners were—probably because he knew no one was even threatening to take his lead.

As Jake flew across the finish line, shouts of "Way to go, Jake!" and "All right, Meadows!"

echoed from the stands. A bunch of guys crowded around to congratulate him. Jake had finished way ahead of the pack.

"Did you see that guy in the gray shorts?" Shannon's screechy voice broke through the celebration in the stands. "What a loser."

Shannon was referring to Curtis Thayer. He had finished last in the heat, well after the other guys.

Shannon really was a jerk. She needed someone to teach her a lesson about sportsmanship. I didn't think I was the person to do it, but obviously no one else was going to do it. I ignored the sick feeling in the pit of my stomach and walked over to Shannon's spot in the front row of the bleachers.

When she saw me, she curled her lip in disgust. "What do you want?" she asked.

I focused an icy stare on her. "You know, all the athletes here tried their best today. It's not very polite to make fun of them." I was sure that everyone could hear my heart pounding. I stepped back and stiffened, waiting for Shannon to let loose with her insults.

Her mouth hung open for a moment. Then she let out a huff of air to show her disgust with me. "Are you talking to me?" she snapped.

That's the worst that Shannon can throw at me? Silent fireworks went off in my head. I had stumped her.

"I think you're being incredibly rude."

Shannon looked me straight in the eyes, her teeth clenched. Neither of us budged.

"Amy!" Claudia called behind me, then grabbed the tail of my T-shirt. "Miss Keller just called your name. You have to get over to the starting line."

My eyes darted back and forth from Claudia to Shannon.

I couldn't keep the other runners waiting.

"Remember, girls, once around the track," Miss Keller said, looking from one seventh-grade girl to the next. "It doesn't sound that far, but it's a tough race. Just do your best." Only six of us were trying out for the team, so this heat would decide which four runners would be Whitman Wildcats.

Sherry was right next to me. "Good luck," she whispered, smiling.

"Thanks," I said, then silently I added, *I'll need it*. I shook my body the way Jake had done, but instead of loosening me up, it just made me more nervous. The knot in my stomach pulled tighter.

Miss Keller backed up onto the grass by the starting line and shouted, "Runners, take your mark!"

We moved into our lanes. A few teachers who had volunteered to keep time lifted their stopwatches.

"Get set!" Each girl wiggled one foot as close to the starting line as possible and bent over. Every nerve in my body felt like an electrical wire sending power through it at top speed.

The shot from the starter's gun exploded in my ear. I sprinted over the starting line as fast as I could. Around the first curve and through the straightaway, I was in the lead.

Suddenly, the muscles in my legs felt like boards. They couldn't take the speed. It took all my power just to make sure they didn't stop completely.

Two of the other girls passed me.

Around the second curve, my legs started to get used to the grueling pace, but I was gasping for every breath. My lungs stung.

Sherry whizzed by. I was in fourth place. As long as no one else passed me, I could still make the team.

Kids and a few parents lined the fence. Above the yells from the sidelines, I heard Jake's friendly voice. "Go, Sherry. You're almost there, Tanya." Then he got louder. "Come on, Amy! You can do better than that."

Jake was right! I couldn't be happy with fourth place, because it wasn't the best I could do.

Faster, I told myself as a hidden burst of energy propelled me down my lane. *Harder!* I inched past the girl in front of me. I turned on the steam and pushed past another runner—coming right up to Sherry, who had taken first place. We were neck and neck. But no matter how hard I struggled, I couldn't move in front of her.

We were only a few feet from the finish line. I lunged forward and managed to cross the line a split second before Sherry.

"Way...to go!" Sherry congratulated me, breathing loudly and clutching her sides as the others patted my back.

"Great race," another voice said.

I looked up, dazed. I could hardly believe that I had finished in first place!

Jake jogged over to me from where he was

standing behind the fence next to Shannon.

"That was awesome! You really came from behind those last fifty yards."

"Thanks for cheering so loud. That really helped."

"Jake, come on," Shannon yelled to her boyfriend. "I have to leave now."

I watched Jake jog back over to Shannon and grab her hand.

Next to them, I noticed Heather waving furiously to get my attention. She had stayed after school for band practice and had promised to come down to the tryouts as soon as practice was over.

"Hey, you made it," I shouted.

"Of course. You didn't think I'd miss seeing my best friend win, did you?"

Dear Diary,

I did it! I'm a Whitman Wildcat! And I broke a school record during my tryout! Life is just about perfect. Of course, it would be more perfect if Rosie and I had been able to patch things up, but I've got to get used to the idea that that will never happen.

And Heather is a great friend. It was really nice to have a real friend cheering for me today.

I'm going to tell her about my period tomorrow. She's my new best friend!

-Amy the track star

(Sorry, I know that sounds conceited!)

Chapter 12

"I wish we could wear our uniforms to practice," Claudia announced, then took a bite of carrot cake. My mother had been so certain that I'd make the team that she'd baked a huge cake in the shape of a track before I got home the day before. It even had little plastic runners on top.

Half of the cake was still left this morning, so I'd brought it to share with Claudia, Sherry, and Heather.

Sherry looked around the cafeteria, then leaned into the center of the table. "I wore mine to bed last night," she told us.

"Not me," I said. "I don't want anything to happen to it before our first meet. I put it right into my drawer." I expected a mocking gasp or sarcastic comment about this uncharacteristic behavior, then realized that none of these girls had ever seen my bedroom. Rosie was the one who always made joking remarks about my messiness.

I looked over at the nearby table where she sat next to Shannon.

"My mom's taking me to the big sale at the mall this weekend," Shannon announced to her friends.

"You should go to Lynette's Fashions," Wendy cut in. "They've got some great sundresses that are way on sale."

Rosie put her chin in her hand and studied the food in front of her. It was strange to see her sitting so quietly as her friends talked about shopping, one of her favorite topics.

Her normally sparkling eyes looked dark and sad. Maybe we weren't friends anymore, but I hated to see her like this. Suddenly Rosie lifted her head and caught me staring. She pushed her lunch tray aside and pretended to be interested in everything Shannon and the other girls said. Occasionally, Rosie gave a fake laugh at one of their remarks.

Then Jake pulled a chair over to the table and sat down next to his girlfriend. Rosie got the weirdest look in her eyes. Shannon kept on talking, and Rosie continued nodding and smiling, but her eyes were fixed on Jake, who tossed a baseball from one hand to the other. When he finally stopped and looked around, Rosie quickly switched her focus back to Shannon.

It didn't take a brain surgeon to figure out what was going on in Rosie's head. She had a crush on Jake—a big one! How long would it take Shannon to figure it out? And if Shannon found *me* threatening, I could only imagine how she'd feel about someone as outgoing and pretty as Rosie.

Of course, whatever happened between Rosie and Shannon was their business. Rosie and I would never get back together—just as my mom and dad never did.

Claudia's words interrupted my thoughts. "Look who's waving at us," she said, tilting her forehead toward the other table. "Jake Meadows."

"He is so cute!" Sherry whispered as we all waved back.

"I think the whole school would agree with you about that," Claudia said once Jake had turned around. "But he's going out with Shannon Sommer." Then Claudia pretended to be

Shannon swinging her long blond hair. Claudia's hair is short, so her imitation was pretty funny.

"I don't know," Sherry said. "I think he has a thing for Amy."

"No way!" I said. "He's just nice."

"Whatever you say," Claudia said. "Anyway, I've got to go. My mom's picking me up for the dentist." She reached for the plastic knife and cut off another piece of cake. "This will be my reward for living through it."

"I'll walk to your locker with you," Sherry said, adjusting a red headband in her black curls. "My next class is on that hall."

When the other two were gone, I looked at the last piece of cake on the table in front of Heather and me. "Want to split it?" I asked.

Heather nodded and cut the piece right down the center. I finished my piece and licked my fingers as Heather wiped a napkin across her mouth.

"Oink!" she said, clutching her stomach and rolling her eyes. Both of us burst out laughing. In practically no time, the four of us had finished off the celebration cake that easily could have fed twice that many.

As our laughter died down, the conversation at the next table drifted over. "Oh, you know how it is. The track team elects their captain, so Jake has to be nice to *everybody*—even if he doesn't really like them," Shannon said loudly.

When I looked up, Shannon was looking directly at me, as though she had wanted me to hear her nasty comment.

Shannon may have been Jake's girlfriend, but she didn't know him very well if she believed that he would be nice to people just because he wanted something.

I thought back to the day I'd seen him help Karen Patel in the lunchroom. She wasn't on the track team. And neither was Heather, and he'd been nice to her.

Unfortunately, I wasn't the only one who had noticed that fact. Shannon went on. "The least he could do is talk to people who know how to dress. Did you notice that mud-brown outfit Heather Midget is wearing today?" The other girls burst into laughter at Shannon's nickname for Heather. "She's got to be the biggest nerd. She doesn't do anything but study."

Heather's cheeks turned bright red, and she stared down at her feet. Tears formed in the corners of her eyes.

I felt horrible. I couldn't just sit there. I

pushed my chair away from the table, walked over to Shannon, and stood in front of her with my arms crossed. Shannon stayed in her chair and studied me from head to toe as though she was examining my clothes.

"Heather is not a nerd," I announced. "She's a much more interesting person than you, and she's ten times nicer besides."

Shannon's friends turned up their noses and curled the corners of their lips.

"Hey, who's she?" Kara asked.

"*That's* Amy Leonard," Wendy explained.

"Get out of here!" Kara snarled.

I stood my ground. If I backed down just because they outnumbered me, Shannon would always think she could attack me and my friends and win.

"Why are you so busy defending Heather? Can't she speak up for herself?" Shannon asked. Then Shannon looked at Wendy and added, "I wonder why her father ran away."

"Her father ran away?" Aaron shouted from the end of the table. A murmur filled the nearby tables as kids began to discuss the rumor.

I can't believe that Shannon is spreading such

vicious lies about Heather! Who does she think she is? I looked over at Heather. She was still staring at the floor, trying to hide her tears.

"Shannon, unless you know the facts, I don't think you should talk about people." The words came out of my mouth before I'd even had a chance to figure out what I was going to say.

"Okay, Amy," she said without flinching. "Tell me the facts."

I could feel the girls at Shannon's table staring at me as they waited for my answer—everyone except Rosie. She shifted nervously in her seat and bit her lip.

I narrowed my eyes at Shannon. "It's none of your business," I told her, clenching my teeth and fists, refusing to tell Heather's secret. I wished I could have thought of something better to say. But it wasn't my place to tell Shannon that Heather's father had died. That was up to Heather.

Shannon stood up, then swung her blond hair over her shoulder. She moved forward so that she was just a few inches in front of me. "It surprises me to hear you say that, since you're always so eager to stick your nose into *my* business."

"What's that supposed to mean?" I asked, standing up straighter. I hoped that the fact that I was three inches taller than she was would intimidate Shannon.

"What's that supposed to mean?" a girl at the table mocked in a singsong voice.

"It means that my friends are mine and you should just stay away." *Her friends.* Who was Shannon talking about? Rosie? Or Jake? Or both?

"I don't think you know what friends are."

"Since I have twice as many friends, I don't need to take any lessons from you," Shannon answered smugly.

"Yeah, well, I wouldn't call *your* friends *real* friends," I announced.

I spun around and walked away. As I got to the end of the table, Shannon called, "That's right. Go back to your loser friends!"

Before I had time to make a decision about my next move, I heard the scrape of a chair scooting away from Shannon's lunch table. One of Shannon's friends was getting up to join her in attacking me.

I turned around and was horrified to see Rosie! Her eyes were round and angry. But instead of looking at me, she was facing Shannon. "You shouldn't go around calling other people's friends losers."

The smug look on Shannon's face turned to pain. "What are you doing?" she whined to Rosie. "I like you, Rosie. You're my friend."

"Well, I'm Amy's friend, too."

"Rosie, what are you talking about?" Shannon squeaked.

"A friend is a friend no matter what," Rosie said firmly. I gave a silent cheer in my head as she continued. "It doesn't matter who they hang out with, or how they dress, or how smart they are." Then she looked at me and smiled. "Real friends don't get jealous." Rosie surveyed Shannon's clique. "You could learn a lot from Amy and Heather," she told them, walking toward me. "I did."

"I thought you were different from them," Shannon said angrily.

"I am different," Rosie said proudly. "The way you guys dress and hold your noses in the air, I can hardly tell you apart."

"I don't have to stay around here and be insulted by you nerds," Shannon huffed. Then she commanded to the girls at her table, "Come on." Like a mother duck and her babies, the popular girls filed out of the lunchroom.

I imagined the entire cafeteria standing and applauding Rosie and me for running Shannon and her gang out of the lunchroom. A few people smiled in my direction, but most of the other kids just went back to their lunches and conversations.

Oh, well, I thought. *At least Rosie's back!*

Chapter 13

"Jake's telling everyone what a great runner you are," Rosie bubbled at the lunch table. "I wish I'd been there to see you."

"Where were you, anyway? I thought you'd come watch with Shannon."

"I was tired of hanging out with her, so I told her I had to go to the environment club meeting."

"The environment club? I didn't know you were into that."

"Neither did I. I had to come up with an excuse, and it was the only thing I could think of. Anyway, I ended up going to the meeting, and I'm going to stay in it. Our advisor, Ms. O'Brien, has a bunch of really cool stuff planned—field trips, community service projects." Rosie's eyes sparkled. "And I kind of got elected president."

"All right!" I cheered.

"Maybe you can use that to get extra credit in science," Heather joked. The last thing Rosie needed was extra credit in science!

Of course, I liked being with Rosie again and talking about track and clubs and stuff. But best friends are supposed to talk about private things. I just wasn't sure how to bring up the subject that was on my mind at that moment: my period.

As I half listened to Rosie and Heather discuss Mr. Norris, I imagined ways to tell Rosie my big news.

Guess what I got! That was no good. Rosie would think I had bought something.

I had a visitor last week. Blech! That sounded too much like something my grandmother would say.

There was also the problem of Heather. Would Rosie mind if I told Heather too? Or should I wait until Rosie and I were alone?

Rosie looked at me, then turned to Heather. "Amy's keeping something from us," she said. "I can tell. She's looks as if she's going to explode."

"Maybe I'm just happy we're all friends."

"No way, Leonard," Rosie protested. "You've

got a big secret. No fair keeping stuff from your best friends."

"Maybe she doesn't think she can trust us," Heather said, pretending to be indignant.

"Okay, okay," I said, more than happy to give in. Both of them leaned forward. "I got my period last week!" I blurted out in a whisper.

Rosie gasped and slapped her hands to her mouth as Heather gave me a high-five.

"That is so excellent," Rosie said once she'd gotten over her shock. "Why didn't you tell me before?" she asked. Everyone at the table became completely silent as I pursed my lips and raised an eyebrow at her. She slumped in her chair and bit her lower lip.

"I'm really sorry about the way I treated both of you—especially about making you sit next to Glen," she apologized.

"Yeah, that was pretty rotten," I said jokingly.

"I never actually meant to be that cruel. Glen overheard me asking Larry Wong to switch seats and volunteered to sit next to you. I didn't know he'd torture you like that."

I looked at Rosie. "You knew Glen liked me?"

"Well, he was pretty obvious about it," she said. "But don't worry. I saw him giving Jeannie

Kim a bouquet of carnations this morning."

"So why'd you change your mind about Shannon?" I asked Rosie.

"Well, at first I really wanted to be popular. Then I found out what Shannon was really like."

"Why didn't you just forget about her and hang out with us?" I asked.

"I was afraid I'd be your second-best friend." Rosie chewed on her lower lip. "I guess I was sort of testing you to see which one of us you liked better."

"You were jealous of *me*?" Heather asked.

"Well, Amy really liked you from the very beginning, and you were good in science. I didn't think Amy needed me anymore."

"I *knew* something else was bothering you. I just didn't know what it was."

"Pretty stupid, huh? I tried to put on a tough act so you wouldn't see how jealous I was. And you didn't seem to care that I had Shannon."

"Are you kidding? I was *really* hurt. I guess I can be pretty stubborn, too. But how could you stand being around those snobby girls, anyway?"

"Well, they were nice to me. And it was pretty fun getting lots of attention and talking about clothes and boys and stuff," Rosie admitted. "But that was *all* we ever discussed. I couldn't tell them the personal stuff we talk about. I was afraid they'd make fun of me the way they did with everyone else."

"Well, now you're way behind in getting to know Heather. I know practically everything about her."

Heather looked sideways at me. "Oh, I don't know. There might just be a few things I haven't told you yet."

A huge smile spread across Rosie's face, and she put her arms around Heather's and my shoulders. "I've got an idea. You can tell your best friends everything—at our sleepover at my house tomorrow night!"

With the three of us as friends, seventh grade was going to be the best year ever!

Dear Diary,
     Thank goodness Rosie came to her senses.
I really missed her. And she just didn't look
right with Shannon Sommer (who detests
us even more now). All the guys still
worship Shannon, and all the girls still want
to be in her group. But now that Rosie's
back, I don't care one bit about Shannon
anymore.
     I don't expect Rosie to give up her

search for popularity, though. As you know, she doesn't give up that easily. There's only one thing better than having Rosie for a best friend—having Rosie and Heather!

—Happy again, Amy

Don't miss the next book in
the Diary S.O.S. series:

I'M GOING TO MEET MY MOTHER

Dear Diary,
Sometimes when I think about being adopted, I feel like I'm falling down a black hole. There are so many thoughts I don't have control over and questions I don't know the answers to. If I had lived with my birth mother, would I play the sax? Would I have friends like Amy and Rosie?

Probably the only way I'll be able to figure anything out is if I meet my birth mother. But sometimes when I look at Mom, meeting Donna seems like a really bad idea. I know Mom's lonely without Dad, and I don't want to make her feel any worse.

I've never kept such a big secret from her, but I don't know what to do.

—Heather

You've met Amy, Heather, and Rosie…
Now meet the girls at the

Jina, Andie, Laurie, and Mary Beth—the four roommates in Suite 4B at Foxhall Academy—may not see eye-to-eye on everything. But they do agree on one thing: they love horses! You'll want to read all the books in this extra-special new series.

#1 • A Horse for Mary Beth

Mary Beth can't wait to get to boarding school. But she never expected that all her classmates would be such serious riders. Trying to fit in, Mary Beth signs up for the junior riding program, but she's absolutely petrified. How will she ever keep her new friends from finding out she's scared of horses?

#2 • Andie Out of Control

Andie Perez loves a challenge—and right now it's to get kicked out of yet another boarding school. She horrifies her roommates by breaking practically every rule in the Foxhall Student Handbook. Then a wild young Thoroughbred named Magic arrives at the school stables, and Andie decides she wants to stay. But it may be too late—for both Andie and Magic!

and coming soon:

#3 • Jina Rides to Win

Jina Williams is one of the best riders at Foxhall Academy. She even boards her own horse at the school stables. Jina knows that she and Superstar can win the Junior Working Hunter Horse of the Year Award. But when she pushes herself and her horse too hard, disaster strikes. Now Jina never wants to ride again...